The Legend of the Serpent Witch

by
F.P. LaRue

Pinckney, Mi

The Legend of the Serpent Witch
Copyright © 2022 F.P. LaRue
All rights reserved by author.

Published by Wynwidyn Press, LLC

This book is a work of fiction. Names, characters, places, and incidents either are products of the author's imagination or are used fictitiously. Any resemblance to actual persons, living or dead, events, or locales is entirely coincidental.

No part of this publication may be reproduced in any form by any means electronic, mechanical, photocopying, recording or otherwise without written permission of the publisher.

For information regarding permission, write to Wynwidyn Press, LLC, and Attention: Permissions Department, 425 Rose St, Pinckney, Michigan, 48169

ISBN: 978-1-941737-36-1

Illustrations and Cover by Darren Wheeling
Interior Book Design by Bob Houston eBook Formatting

This book is dedicated to those who love adventuring -- no matter what their age!

Acknowledgments

I would like to thank the following people for their invaluable help in the creation, editing and publishing of this book. Your assistance is sincerely appreciated.

- Robin Moyer
- Darren Wheeling
- Marlo Garnsworthy
- Kelly Kiefer
- Darci Ravenscraft

CHAPTER 1

I have a true story to tell you. I don't know if you'll believe it or not. But it really happened. I swear on the heads of my two best friends, Mellie and Scotty. I would never have believed it if I didn't experience it myself. Thinking back on it, I wonder if we could have handled things any differently? I don't know. You be the judge.

It started one day when I was walking through the woods near my school. There is a shortcut in the woods that I use. It's quicker than going around the woods to get home. I go this way a lot. I like being in the woods and pretending that I'm protecting my family, friends, and town against evil forces that want to destroy them.

My name is Oliver, Ollie to my friends. I'm twelve years old. I've been told that I have a big heart. I don't know about that. I've also been told that I have a sixth sense about things. I don't even know what that means. It may mean I have a sense of when something is not quite right. I'm not sure. I know that I'm very curious by nature and have wanted to solve mysteries my whole life. I consider myself the best investigator that ever lived. Well, at least, I would like to be.

I love my town. It can be very peaceful. Most of the time, though, it's very boring. But every once in a while, something happens to threaten that peace and the families here. I always want to be ready in case that happens. I didn't know it at the time, but a mystery was already happening, and I would be involved.

But on that day, I was just enjoying being in the woods. I was thinking about an experiment I wanted to do in my workroom, later when I got home.

I have my own workroom in my basement. I try to create concoctions and powders that I can use to combat evildoers who threaten my town. I think of myself as the Evil Destroyer.

At the time, I was working on a special powder that would stun the evildoer enough that I could get the upper hand in any situation. Or at least give me a chance to run away. I call it Stun and Run. I was making progress, but it wasn't perfected yet. I wanted to continue working on it.

As I was walking, I noticed a scarf caught on a bush on the side of the path. It was brown with green leaves on it. The day was cloudy and overcast. The wind had picked up, and the scarf was fluttering in the breeze.

It was similar to one that I used to have. *Some kid lost his scarf,* I thought. I quickly forgot about it . . . .

But the next day, I took the same path and noticed something stuck on a branch. This time it was a baseball cap.

Looks like another kid lost something, I thought. Kids lose things all the time.

The Legend of the Serpent Witch

I pulled the baseball cap off the branch. It was blue, with a yellow lightning bolt. It looked pretty cool. I tried it on.

This fits pretty well, I thought. For a second, I considered taking it. Then I reasoned that the kid who lost it might come back to find it. If it were my cap, I'd hope the person who found it would just leave it, so I could get it back. I decided to put it back on the branch.

As I walked away, I glanced down, and something caught my attention. Being the best investigator who has ever lived, I have an eye for detail. I wasn't sure what I was seeing, but there appeared to be drag marks in the dirt. I looked a little closer. I could see shoe prints. Then right after that, round indentations in the dirt. Yes. They looked like heel marks. It was as if someone, or something, had been dragged through this area.

That can't be right, I reasoned.

I bent down to examine them closer. They sure looked like drag marks, and they led deeper into the woods.

What's going on here? I asked. *Who or what was dragged into the woods? And why would they need to be dragged in the first place?*

I started to feel a little creepy. I looked around to make sure I was alone. Everything seemed OK. I followed the marks, hoping to find some answers. I followed them for a hundred feet or so. Then there was nothing but dead leaves and twigs on the ground leading up to a large tree. The marks seemed to just disappear in the woods.

I stared at the ground. *Where did the marks go?*

I didn't see any drag marks anywhere. There were only undisturbed leaves and twigs.

That can't be right, I thought again. I must have missed something somewhere. Or maybe, kids were just playing around. I scanned the area once more for any marks, but there was nothing. I shrugged and kept going.

CHAPTER 2

On the third day, my best friends in the world, Mellie and Scotty, were with me as we were walking to school.

When I think about them, I always smile. Sometimes they aggravate me, but I don't know what I'd do without them. We swore an oath years ago to always help each other and cover each other's back. We put our fists together and vowed to be friends forever. Anyway, I know I can count on them to be there if I need them.

Mellie is a bookworm. She is very intelligent. I don't know if she's cute or not. I just know I like her. She is level-headed and tries to see the logic behind everything. If she doesn't understand something, she tries to find answers by using facts, not hearsay. She doesn't believe in anything she can't see or feel. That can come in handy when solving mysteries.

Scotty, on the other hand, has a big imagination. When he gets nervous, he takes off or adjusts his glasses. He's kind of a chicken when it comes to scary stuff, but he does what he has to do in the end, even if he doesn't want to. I know I can count on him to do the right thing, even if he's scared or wants to run away. At least, in most cases. He is open-minded to anything, even the supernatural.

We walked for a while along the path. I was looking for the scarf and baseball cap I saw yesterday. I didn't see either one. I didn't see anything unusual at all. Mellie and Scotty were talking about school, just regular stuff about teachers and other students. Then Mellie noticed something. Some gloves were sticking out from under a small rock. Mellie bent over to pick up the gloves. They were medium sized and were black with a green stripe on each of the fingers, that connected at the top of the glove.

"Hey," said Mellie. "Do these belong to anyone? They look like something you would wear."

"Not mine," said Scotty.

"This is strange," I said.

"What's so strange about gloves?" asked Mellie. "They're just gloves." She picked them up and looked at them. She put them back where she found them and put the rock back on top.

"I don't know," I said. "But I don't remember seeing so many things on this path before. Maybe it's nothing, but it just seems strange to find another piece of clothing here."

"What do you mean?" asked Mellie curiously.

"This is the third thing, all in the same area," I said.

"Third thing? What else did you find?" asked Scotty.

I told them about the scarf and baseball cap.

"And look at this." I pointed to a tree near the gloves. The tree branch looked broken. As if someone tried to grab onto it and it broke.

"That doesn't necessarily mean anything," said Scotty. He was starting to look a little concerned as he touched the branch.

"Scotty is right. That doesn't mean anything," said Mellie, waving her hand in dismissal. "Many kids use this path."

"Yeah," said Scotty, "the wind just probably blew the baseball cap and scarf here. Same with the gloves. Or someone just dropped them."

"I know what you're saying, but I don't think so," I said. "Maybe someone dropped them, or the wind blew the baseball cap and scarf here. But the gloves were under a rock! I have a feeling something's going on. Something's not right."

"Here he goes again," said Scotty, rolling his eyes. "Wanting to solve a mystery."

"Quit seeing a mystery where there isn't one," said Mellie. "We'll come back here tomorrow and see if there's anything else. I doubt it, though." She shook her head.

"Your imagination is way too active, Ollie," joked Scotty.

I didn't say anything. I just looked around suspiciously. I was starting to feel concerned. *I hope they're right*, I thought, trying to ignore the slight twinge of uneasiness I felt growing in my stomach.

I thought about what I had found in the woods. It's just some kids that lost some clothing. Maybe Mellie and Scotty were right.

There's nothing to even think about. There's no problem here. Maybe my imagination *was* getting away from me. I shook my head, starting to feel foolish.

But then I remembered the drag marks. *What about them?*

The Legend of the Serpent Witch

No matter how I tried to explain the situation away, I still had an uneasy feeling throughout the day. I couldn't get rid of it.

CHAPTER 3

After school, I went back to where I'd found the scarf and baseball cap. They still weren't there. I looked around, but I didn't see anything unusual. Everything seemed normal, everything as it should be.

I sighed out loud. *What's my problem*? Was I seeing sinister things when there weren't any? *All of this can be easily explained*, I told myself. But what was the explanation? I shook my head, perplexed. Why was I so concerned about a few items left in the woods? Probably not even left in the woods but maybe blown in by the wind.

"Am I so desperate for a mystery that I'm making one up?" I asked out loud. I looked at the trees, then at the ground, as if hoping they would give me an answer. They didn't. All was quiet.

Eerily quiet… Stop that, I thought.

All of a sudden, I heard something. Or I thought I heard something. It sounded like someone or something was breathing. But it couldn't be, because I was all alone.

"Come on," I said. "Now you're spooking yourself into

hearing things."

But I heard it again. It was very faint. I peered into the thick forest. I listened intently. I was almost afraid to move in case I made a noise and missed it. Whatever *it* was. I was holding my breath and didn't realize it until I had to exhale.

What is it? It wasn't the wind. It wasn't an animal. It sounded creepy, whatever it was.

There, it goes again. I put my hand behind my ear, as if that would help me hear better. I don't know why I did that. I think I saw it on some scary TV show somewhere.

It was slightly louder this time. I couldn't quite make it out. It sounded like… I strained to hear it. I could almost make it out… like the wind was moaning, like a faint voice saying, "Oh way."

Oh way? I thought. *What does that mean? That can't be right.* I shook my head.

Then something whispered, "Go away!" It sounded right next to my ear! I swung around; my arms raised to protect myself.

Nothing was there!

"Go away!" the voice whispered again. This time next to my other ear.

My body jerked with fear. That's all I needed to hear. I took off running so fast that I was surprised that I didn't leave my shoes behind. I didn't look back, afraid of what I'd see.

CHAPTER 4

The next day, I decided I would put my fear behind me and go back to the woods. I really needed to see if I could make any sense of all this. Sometimes being the best investigator out there is hard.

After school, I met with Mellie and Scotty, and we walked to the woods. I told them about the tracks and that it had looked like something, or someone had been dragged deeper into the woods. They thought I was really letting my imagination run wild.

Mellie and Scotty teased me about finding the scarf and baseball cap in the woods. "Maybe we'll find something scary like boots," laughed Scotty.

"Or something that will give us all nightmares, like socks!" giggled Mellie.

Scotty and Mellie were joking, pushing, and nudging me in a way only friends can do. I took it good-naturedly and thought maybe they were right. There was nothing to be concerned about. The wind was responsible for what I thought I heard. And it also blew in the items we'd found. That's all there was to it. I started feeling better about the whole thing.

But when we reached the clearing where I'd found the scarf, the scarf that hadn't been there yesterday was back!

"That wasn't here yesterday afternoon," I exclaimed. "I came back to the woods to look for it."

"Are you sure?" asked Scotty.

"Yes, I'm sure," I said.

I picked up the brown scarf with green leaves on it. "This is what I saw a couple of days ago."

I was sure because, this particular bush was shaped differently than the others, a little smaller and less leafy.

I checked for the drag marks but couldn't find any. All I saw was dirt, grass, and dead leaves.

"Come on," I said and made my way to where I found the blue baseball cap.

"It's there, too!" It was the same one with the yellow lightning bolt I saw the other day. "And it's in the exact same place I first found it."

"These weren't here yesterday," said Mellie. She was perplexed.

"What's going on?" Scotty scratched his head and took off his glasses.

"I don't know," I said. "It's very odd for this scarf and baseball cap, which were here two days ago but not here yesterday, to be here again today. The same scarf and baseball cap, in the same place."

"Maybe it's just a coincidence," Scotty said hopefully, putting his glasses back on.

"That's an awfully big coincidence," said Mellie. She shook her head not ready to accept that idea.

"Let's go and see if the gloves are still there," I said, though I had a sinking feeling that they wouldn't be. I thought they might have disappeared like the scarf and baseball cap.

We arrived at the spot where we had seen the gloves. I looked down. Then I glanced at Mellie and Scotty. They were staring at me, at each other, and the ground.

Sure enough, the gloves were gone. *They could have been blown away by the wind,* I thought. But I really didn't think so. They had been under a rock.

"What's going on?" asked Scotty. He scanned the area quickly, nervously.

"Someone is trying to tell us something," I said.

"But what?" asked Mellie.

"It could be a warning," I suggested. "Someone wanted us to find those things." I pointed back to where the baseball cap and scarf were located.

"Then what? They wanted us to notice that the gloves are now missing?" asked Mellie. She clearly couldn't understand the logic behind it.

"Why would someone do that?" asked Scotty, shaking his head. "It doesn't make sense."

"I agree," Mellie said, scratching her head.

"I don't know what's going on here," I said. "But I bet it makes some sick, twisted sense to someone. And there's something else… I thought I heard something weird in the woods yesterday."

"Like what?" asked Mellie nervously.

"It sounded like 'Go away'," I said.

"'Go away?' What does th-that mean?" stuttered Scotty. "Why should you go away?" He raised his arm, palm up, agitated.

"I don't know," I said, "I was walking through the woods to where I saw the scarf and baseball cap. I thought I heard something. It sounded far away, but it still sounded creepy. I kept listening but wasn't sure what it was. Then someone or something whispered, 'Go away.' I didn't see anyone or anything."

"Who would want you to 'go away?'" asked Mellie. She sounded like she wanted to know, but at the same time didn't want to know.

"I don't know that either," I said. "But it scared me enough that I did 'go away.' I ran all the way home... FAST! I swear my shoes were smoking when I got home." I stepped up and down quickly as if my shoes were on fire.

Mellie and Scotty laughed at that. Scotty touched his shoe like it was hot and smoking. He blew on his finger and waved his hand over his shoe as if to cool down the smoke.

After we discussed it for a while, Scotty said, as he cleaned his glasses, "Seriously, though, I don't like this."

"It is a little strange and creepy." Mellie shivered and rubbed her arms.

"I agree," I said. "Something's not right. I have a feeling someone needs help—our help."

We all looked around anxiously.

I stared at the woods, as if waiting for it to give me some answers.

Mellie peered up at the sky. She looked like she was searching for possible explanations.

Scotty gazed at the ground. He was shaking his head and fidgeting with his glasses. "I don't know what we have gotten ourselves into this time," he said. "But whatever it is, it can't be good…especially for us."

I looked at Scotty and Mellie. They seemed really uptight, concentrating so hard to figure things out. I thought that maybe we needed a break. We needed to get our minds off these strange events. There was one thing that would help distract us.

"Anyone want some candy?" I asked.

Mellie and Scotty smiled.

"Great idea," Mellie said.

"I'll race you guys over there," said Scotty, as he started to run to town, toward the candy shop. Thankfully, it wasn't far away.

CHAPTER 5

Scotty beat us to the candy shop. We were laughing when we got there, already feeling better.

The candy shop was owned by Aggie. She was very friendly, and everyone liked her. She smiled at us when we came in. We waved at her. She always looked nice, even when wearing an apron that was constantly messed up with candy smudges on it. Even as we walked in, she was wiping her hands on her apron. Every once in a while, she'd add a little extra candy to an order when a kid looked like they were having a bad day.

Her shop was always fun because it had pictures, toys, and puzzles for kids to look at while they waited. It was a great place for kids to go if they had a hard day at school. Whatever it was, trouble with a classmate, a problem with a teacher, or just having worries on their mind, a visit to the candy shop was a sure-fire way to feel better.

Aggie was waiting on a customer when we went in. When she finished, she asked what she could get us.

We had been looking over all the different types of candies.

"I'll have the chocolate with nuts candy bar, please," I said.

"I'll have the white chocolate triangle candy, please," said

Mellie.

Aggie patiently waited for Scotty to make his selection.

"I'll have the chocolate, caramel, peanut butter crunch, please. With a little whipped cream on it," Scotty added.

Mellie and I looked at him a bit surprised and smiled at his order.

"What?" Scotty asked.

We all started to laugh. For the moment, for Mellie and Scotty, everything was right in our world again. Unfortunately, I still had that sense of uneasiness that wouldn't leave me.

CHAPTER 6

The next day, Mellie called Scotty and me to come over to her home. Her house was similar to the other houses on the block. The living room and kitchen faced the street. We sat at the kitchen table. Everything was neat and clean. She already had her computer on.

"I found an article about two kids in our area that have run away," Mellie explained, "and so far, no one has been able to locate them. I don't know if this has anything to do with what we found, but I thought we should check it out."

I skimmed one article she had discovered. "This article reports that the two missing boys were last seen in town buying candy at the candy shop. It was thought that they went through the woods after buying their candy, though their ultimate destination was unknown. It describes what the boys looked like and the clothes they were wearing."

As I kept skimming, nothing stood out, but then I stopped and raised my head.

Mellie looked at me questioningly.

"What is it?" asked Scotty.

"The article mentions one boy had a blue baseball cap, and the other boy had a brown scarf." I shook my head. *Could this be a coincidence?* I pondered. *This just can't be right.*

"What about the gloves?" Mellie asked.

"There's no mention of any gloves," I said. "The article says the police have already checked out the woods where the two boys could have gone. They found a trail they might have taken. There were tracks on the trail. Then the tracks just vanished. The police didn't think that was unusual, with all the wind and rain that happened at the time. It wouldn't have taken long for any tracks to disappear."

We sat quietly, trying to make sense of it all.

"I can't believe two boys are just missing in our town," Scotty said. "That just doesn't happen here."

"Yeah, that's what I thought, too," said Mellie. "But as I was researching them, I expanded my search from our town to some surrounding towns. It's not as rare as you might think."

Then Mellie started to read through the other articles. Finally, pointing at the screen, she said, "Look at this." There were a few articles about kids going missing over several years. At first, it didn't seem like a large number of disappearances. But added up over time, there were a noticeable number of them. The names of some of the missing kids were mentioned, along with some of their personal items; toys, books, and things like that. Things they had with them when they disappeared. Despite multiple searches for the kids, nothing was ever found. The disappearances were never really explained. Most people in the communities, thought that they were runaways and eventually, they made their way home. As time went by, they were forgotten about.

Mellie sat back from the computer. "Why are these cases unexplained?" she asked, shaking her head.

"Maybe they all did make it home," suggested Scotty. "These disappearances happened over a long period of time."

"I know. But still…" I said. "And what about the two who went missing not all that long ago? I checked the internet for information about them, but couldn't find anything useful. I would feel better knowing that they are all right."

"Me too," said Scotty.

"Same here," said Mellie.

She continued to read the article. "It was thought that the children might have run away. In most of the cases, they probably went back home, or their parents know where they are," Mellie said. "The article just left it at that."

"This just doesn't sound right." From the expressions on their faces, I could see they were thinking the same thing.

"I can't understand why more wasn't done at the time," said Mellie.

"I know what you mean," said Scotty. "We must be missing something here that might explain what happened to them."

A feeling of dread started to come over me.

I just wasn't satisfied with what we found on the internet. We needed to get more information. I suggested that we go to the library. The library might have more information, or the librarian may suggest other tools than the internet.

"That's a great idea," said Mellie. "Maybe we can find more

detailed information there."

Scotty agreed. "Maybe the information we find there can help answer some of our questions."

"Before we go to the library, let's stop and get the scarf and baseball cap," I suggested. "We should give them to the police, just in case they did belong to the two runaways. We don't want them to disappear again."

"That's a good idea," said Mellie.

"The scarf and baseball cap may not be theirs," Scotty said hopefully.

Mellie and I just stared disbelievingly at him.

"But they should be checked out," he said finally.

But when we went back to the woods to get the scarf and baseball cap…

…they were gone!

Of course, they are, I thought.

CHAPTER 7

Our library is like any other small-town library. It has all kinds of books in different areas. It is very comfortable, and I always enjoy going there. Our librarian, Cassandra, was very friendly and helpful. She's a lot older than us, but I guess she's still considered young—for an adult. She wore long dresses with flower designs and kept her hair pulled back in a bun. She had been there less than a year, but she fit right in. She replaced our other librarian, who left quickly without saying where she was going or why she was leaving. She just kind of disappeared. People said maybe she had to take care of elderly relatives in another state, but nobody knew for sure.

When we went into the library, Cassandra was helping a parent find a picture book for their child. When she was finished, we asked her to help us find articles or stories about any missing children in our area.

"Well, let me see," she said curiously, touching her chin. "Let's go over to the computer section." We followed her over to one of the computers. She scrolled through articles on the Internet. "Here's an article about two runaways not too long ago," she said.

"I found that article already," said Mellie. "Are there any others?"

"Hmm, I'm not sure. Let's see," said Cassandra. She found the articles Mellie read about other unexplained disappearances.

Mellie explained that she had already found those as well.

Cassandra gave her a surprised look. She continued to scan various articles, but she couldn't find anything to help us out. "We do have archives that you could check to see about any disappearances," she suggested.

"That would be great, checking out the archives' older articles may be just what we need," I said.

Cassandra left us to study the archives. While searching the archives, we confirmed that children had disappeared, not only in our town but in other cities and towns as well.

Still, I just couldn't believe so many kids had disappeared over the years. "What happened to them?" I asked. "It must be like what we read before. The kids were thought to be runaways and that they returned home at some time."

"It does seem like they were just forgotten about as time went on," Mellie said.

"What is this?" I asked.

Mellie and Scotty waited expectantly.

"Here is one explanation for the disappearances. It sounds kind of unbelievable. I've never heard about this before."

"What is it?" Mellie asked curiously.

"Did we miss something?" asked Scotty.

I told them what I found. "Here's an article called *The*

Legend of the Serpent Witch. This happened many, many years ago. It's a story about an evil witch that the townspeople were afraid of. They thought she could do black magic. They banished her to the woods surrounding the town. Every once in a while, a kid would go missing. The townspeople searched for them, but they were never found. The townspeople blamed it on the evil Serpent Witch, even though they had no proof that the witch did anything to the kids."

We were so absorbed in what we were reading we didn't hear Cassandra come up behind us.

"What are you kids reading about? Did you find what you were looking for?" she asked, standing behind us.

Cassandra so surprised us, I almost jumped out of my seat.

Mellie grabbed my chair to keep from falling off hers.

"What?" Scotty squeaked in surprise.

"I asked, did you find what you were looking for?" Cassandra was trying not to smile at our reactions.

"I don't know" I said. "But I have a question for you. Do you know about an evil Serpent Witch that was said to be responsible for children disappearing?"

"Well, I'm not sure," she said, pushing a loose strand of hair behind her ear. "Let me see what you're reading about." She scanned the article. "Oh yes, I have heard this story. It's a myth, but some people swore it was true. It's been a long time since I heard this story. Please go on, Ollie." Cassandra was listening intently.

I continued to read about the Serpent Witch.

"It was a long time ago, of course. There was a girl in the

village who was supposedly cursed from birth. No one could remember how that all came about. But because she was cursed, they thought she was evil and a witch. The girl grew up to be an ugly child. The villagers made fun of her. They would hit her and throw stones at her. It was said that snakes were drawn to her ugliness and evil. She made them her pets. They were her only friends. Her snakes were always around wherever she was. She was never without them.

"Ew, snakes as pets!" said Mellie. "That's gross."

"At least they're not spiders," Scotty said.

"As she grew older, she hated the townspeople and wanted to get back at them," I continued. "She would leave gifts or food to lure kids to a clearing in the woods. Once there, she would trick them into thinking that she liked them and wanted to give them more gifts. She would cry, and the children felt sorry for her.

"According to the legend, they would follow her to her hut, where she would give them treats and water. The water was sweet because she put a potion made of snake venom and honey into it. It made them fall asleep and then become paralyzed. The last thing the kids would see was her ugly face laughing with glee at their horror as she said what she was going to do to them. And even worse, what her pet snakes would do to them."

Cassandra shook her head and whispered, "It's just a myth."

"The Serpent Witch would catch the kids' last breaths in jars," I said. "She would breathe in their youth and goodness from the jars."

At this point, Cassandra chuckled. "Breathe in their youth and goodness from jars. That's my favorite part," she joked. "Remember, it's all just a myth."

Cassandra saw another parent and child motioning to her that they needed help. Mellie, Scotty, and I must have looked nervous because she said, "I have better ghost stories for you than this. They're in the fiction section." She laughed as she walked away to help the patrons.

"Their youth and goodness made her pretty," I said. "They helped her to stay young for years and years. It was said she killed many children over the centuries. Over time, she seemed to disappear and was never heard of again. It was thought that she was long dead."

"I hope so," whispered Scotty.

"Cassandra is right. It's probably just a myth," Mellie said, doubt in every word.

"We should be that lucky," I said wistfully.

We just looked at each other in disbelief. *Could this be true?* I wondered, knowing the answer intuitively, but not wanting to believe it. If it was true, it happened in the past. *It doesn't mean it's happening now,* I reasoned.

Mellie just stared straight ahead, a concerned expression on her face.

Scotty swallowed nervously. "We don't have anything to worry about. If it is the Serpent Witch and she breathed in the 'goodness' of some of the kids here, she'd get sick," he joked.

Mellie gave a half-hearted laugh.

The Legend of the Serpent Witch

I smiled but wondered what was really going on.

"This is so strange," I said. "There's a legend about an evil witch who took children for their youth and goodness. Now we have kids who are missing. And unexplained disappearances that have been going on for quite some time. Is this all connected?" I asked. "Can't be. Right? Sounds crazy. Right?"

They said nothing.

But I thought, *Still...*

CHAPTER 8

The next afternoon, we met at the edge of the woods. Mellie and Scotty were unusually quiet.

"I'm not sure what's going on, but this seems to be the best place to start," I said.

Mellie and Scotty nodded hesitantly; anxiety written all over their faces. Mellie seemed like she wanted to say something but couldn't. Scotty was searching around like he wanted to find a place to hide. I understood their worry. I was worried, too. I just didn't know what else to do.

Something was wrong here. We had to find out what. "If you're stuck, keep moving forward, I always say. Let's go."

"When did he ever say that?" asked Mellie.

"Who knows?" said Scotty as they reluctantly followed me.

We made our way to where we had found the clothing. We started with where I had first seen the scarf. Mellie pointed to where it had been. It wasn't there now. Then we went to where I'd found the baseball cap. It wasn't there either. Nor were the gloves under the rock. There were no drag marks either.

We checked the surrounding area, but we couldn't find

anything that wasn't supposed to be there. There was nothing unusual at all that we could see.

"OK, first, I found the scarf and baseball cap and the drag marks. Then they weren't there, but the gloves were there, and the branch was broken," I said, trying to make sense of it. "Then the scarf and baseball cap were there again, but the gloves were gone. Now everything is missing. This is all very strange."

"It is strange, but everything seems to be OK now," said Scotty with a sigh of relief. "Nothing to worry about now."

"Scotty is right," said Mellie. "Looks like a dead end."

"I guess you're right," I said.

When we turned to leave, an unusually strong, creepy feeling came over me. I can't really explain it except to say that it stopped me in my tracks.

"What's wrong?" asked Mellie, bumping into me.

"Why did we stop?" asked Scotty as he almost knocked into Mellie.

Then everything got very quiet. It was so quiet that the only thing I heard was Mellie and Scotty's breathing. I swear that I could hear their hearts beating as fast as mine. There seemed to be no air in the woods. Time appeared to stop as if it were afraid to continue. I felt like we were waiting for something terrible to happen. Whatever it was, it was coming our way.

"Ollie?" whispered Scotty.

I turned to him.

Then Mellie whispered, "What's going on?"

Just then, I smelled a sickeningly sweet odor.

"Do you guys smell that?" I asked.

They didn't have a chance to respond. We were suddenly surrounded by dark gray smoke. I quickly turned around, trying to figure out what was going on. The dark smoke whirled and spun quickly between us. I could feel it on my skin. It felt like icy fingertips with long, sharp, jagged nails touching us. I didn't know what was happening. I shook with cold and fright.

I couldn't see Mellie or Scotty. Or anything around me, only the smoke.

"Hey, you guys?" I called out. There was no response. Then I felt something wet and sticky on my skin.

I put my arm out and touched something. Mellie screamed, not knowing it was me.

"Grab my hand if you can," I yelled, "and then grab Scotty's hand."

"OK!" Mellie shouted, relieved that I was going to help her. She quickly grabbed my hand.

"Scotty, grab my hand!" she screamed.

"Where are you?" Scotty shouted in disgust and terror. "Something is licking me!"

"I'm reaching for your ..." Mellie screamed, but she stopped abruptly.

"Oliver! Something ice cold and slippery wrapped itself around my hand," she shrieked in horror.

I tugged hard to pull Mellie close to me.

"It let go of me," Mellie shouted in relief.

Somehow, Mellie grabbed Scotty's hand. "I have him!" she yelled.

The Legend of the Serpent Witch

We tried to escape the dark gray smoke whirling around us by running through it, but there was a force of some kind holding us inside it.

"At the count of three," I yelled, "everyone push toward me as hard as you can." I didn't give them time to think about it. We had to get out of this dark gray smoke. "One, two, three… push!"

We pushed our way out of the spinning smoke and fell crashing to the ground. I had a tingling feeling through my body that made the hairs on my arms stand straight up. One minute we were in the whirling dark gray smoke; the next minute, we were flat on the ground. The smoke was gone.

We just lay on the ground for a few minutes. I tried to catch my breath. Mellie and Scotty did, too.

After a while, I asked, "Did you smell that awful stink before?"

"I didn't smell anything," Mellie said.

"Me neither," said Scotty.

I thought for a second… "Oh well… I want to tell you something," I said. "This is going to sound strange—"

"Couldn't be any stranger than what just happened," interrupted Scotty.

Mellie nodded.

"Well, when I counted to three, it felt like someone or something helped push me out," I said, feeling a little confused.

"Of course, it did," said Mellie. "Scotty and I were both pushing with everything we had."

Scotty nodded.

"Well… not exactly pushed. It was more like pulled," I said. "It felt like a hand grabbed me and helped pull me out as you guys were pushing. But thinking about it, it couldn't be. There was nothing there. Nothing I could see, anyway."

One at a time, we sat up.

I looked at Mellie and Scotty to make sure they were all right. Everything happened so fast.

"Did we just imagine that?" Mellie asked.

"Maybe we were dreaming," suggested Scotty. "I can't believe what just happened."

I stared at them in shock.

They stared back at me.

"I don't think we were dreaming," I said, pointing to their arms. They were pointing at me. They were so dazed they couldn't talk.

Our hands and arms were wet and were covered with red welts!

CHAPTER 9

What just happened? I asked myself. None of us could believe what we had just experienced. "Are you guys OK?" I asked Mellie and Scotty.

Mellie said, "I think so."

"I'm not sure," said Scotty. "I'll have to get back to you."

After a while, we started to calm down. I said, "Whatever had happened was over. We'll be OK." After a few minutes, everything seemed normal again, well, kind of.

We were worried about what to say to our parents about the welts. "Our parents are going to see these welts and ask us what happened," I said. "We're going to have to come up with some story to tell them."

"You're right," Mellie agreed.

"They're ugly, but at least they don't hurt," Scotty commented, as he examined his arms.

We were grateful about that. We knew our parents wouldn't believe how we really got them, and we didn't want them to tell us not to go into the woods, so we wouldn't get hurt again.

"Looks like we don't have to come up with a story after all,"

I said. "Our problem solved itself." I smiled as I pointed to Mellie and Scotty's arms. To our relief, as our hands and arms dried, the welts just disappeared. It was as if they never existed.

We didn't know what had just happened. But we wanted to find out. At least, I wanted to find out. Mellie and Scotty wanted to find out, too; they just didn't want to find out firsthand. But, as usual, they were good sports. Plus, they didn't want me to investigate on my own.

We needed to do something. What? I didn't know. But I knew that what happened to us, the runaways, and the woods were somehow connected. I thought we should at least investigate and see what we could find.

"Mellie, Scotty, remember the article on the recent runaways?" I asked. "It said they were last seen at the candy shop. Maybe we should ask Aggie if she remembers seeing them and if she can tell us anything that might help."

Mellie and Scotty agreed.

When we went to the candy shop, Aggie was cleaning the counter. She waved. "Scotty, Mellie, Ollie, how are we doing today?"

"Aggie, there is something we want to ask you about," I said. I was hoping Aggie might remember something that would help us figure out what was happening.

"Yes, what is it?" she asked.

"Do you remember the two missing kids that came in here a while back?" I asked.

"Yes, of course. I remember them," she replied. She was very responsive to my questions. "They ordered some candy, were talking to each other, and left," she explained. "They said they were going to meet with some friends down the street, and then they were going to cut through the woods and go adventuring. It sounded like they were going to have fun. They also said they liked the toys and the pictures of kids playing games displayed here in the shop. I gave them their candy, and they left. That's the last I heard of them until the police came and asked about them." She shrugged.

Aggie helped a customer who came into the candy shop. When she finished with that customer, she came back to us and said, "I hope they're OK." She had a worried expression on her face. "If there were any way I could help, I would."

"Well, Evil Destroyer, it looks like a dead end," said Mellie.

"Evil Destroyer?" Aggie asked curiously.

"That's what Ollie calls himself," said Mellie. "He wants to protect us from anyone or anything that is evil and would threaten us."

"Unfortunately, I don't know what kind of evil we're facing now," I said.

When she saw the worried looks we gave each other, Aggie tried to make us feel better. She smiled. "I don't think there is anything to be concerned about here," she assured us. "I'm sure they're OK by now. They are probably home with their parents safe and sound."

"I hope she's right," I said as we left the candy shop. "The boys mentioned that they were going to cut through the woods and go adventuring. Maybe they didn't make it through the woods. Maybe they came across something or someone that prevented them from leaving the woods."

"What are you saying, Ollie?" Scotty asked anxiously.

"You're not thinking about that Serpent Witch myth, are you?" asked Mellie, disbelief and concern written all over her face.

"Or that gray smoke stuff?" added Scotty.

"I don't know what I'm thinking." I shook my head, trying to get a clear understanding of what was happening. "But what I do know is that we have to go back to the woods." I wasn't sure what we were going to do there. "I just know that the key to solving this mystery is connected to the woods."

Before we left for the woods, I said I wanted to stop by my house first. I went in and put a bag of the Stun and Run powder that I had been working on in my pocket.

I told Mellie and Scotty what I had done. "It's not perfected yet, but it may come in handy if we need to get away from someone or something. Anyway… just in case."

"That's a good idea," said Mellie.

"Let's hope we don't have to use it. Let's go before it starts to get dark," Scotty said, nervously scanning about for anything or anyone who might be dangerous.

"Agreed," said Mellie.

As we went back into the woods, I was lost in my thoughts. Mellie looked like she was concentrating hard on what we knew. Scotty seemed like he was thinking about something scary. His eyes were wide and his hands were trembling.

I was scared but determined. I felt Mellie and Scotty were, too, each in their own way. I knew that if we could help those missing kids in some way, we were going to do it.

CHAPTER 10

When we got to the woods, we first searched the areas where we found the pieces of clothing and the drag marks. We found nothing out of sorts. Then we expanded our search area. A few hundred feet away we came upon a clearing with several large rocks. We decided to regroup and sat on the rocks facing each other.

"Let's go over what we know," I said. "First of all, according to the myth, the kids went into the woods. The witch was in the woods. Kids disappeared from the woods. Now, in the present day, the missing kids went through the woods. The items we found, which were probably theirs, were in the woods. The kids are now missing. Everything centers around the woods."

"That's right," said Mellie.

"There's no getting around any of that," agreed Scotty reluctantly.

The only problem was that one part concerned a myth, and the other part was real. We didn't really want to believe that an evil witch from centuries ago could really be here, now, in our woods. There must be some other explanation, but we couldn't come up with anything that sounded right. We discussed some more but seemed to be going in circles. We went back and forth between the myth and what was happening now. After a while, we stopped speculating because we weren't accomplishing anything.

It was starting to get dark, so we decided to head back home. Just as we turned to leave, a dark shadow appeared before us. It was nearly dusk, and the sun was not strong enough to cast such a dark shadow.

I jumped back, grabbing hold of Mellie and Scotty. They jumped back, too, holding on to me and each other. I felt their muscles tighten. They were ready to run. The shadow was just standing there. Not moving.

After a few seconds, with the shadow not moving, I let go of Mellie and Scotty. Mellie still held onto my arm. Scotty had his hand on my back, gripping my shirt with his fist. I peered at the dark shadow more closely.

I could barely make out what it was. It looked like an old woman. She wore a black cloak with a hood. I started to take a breath and felt a little relieved. Then she stepped in front of us to block our way.

She carried a long, bone-colored stick. I could barely see her face. It looked kind of stern. I got the impression she was angry. At us? What did we do? I didn't know. I wasn't sure I wanted to find out either.

For a moment, no one said anything. As the old woman took a step toward us, we moved backward, unsure what to expect.

I didn't feel good about this, but I asked, "Who are you?" My voice was shaking. I was trying hard not to show how scared I was.

I couldn't see her eyes, but I knew she was staring intently at us. I felt the intensity of her stare. I felt like it was penetrating straight through my eyes into my skull. It didn't feel good.

We just stood there, not knowing what to do. When it didn't seem like she was going to answer, I turned to Mellie and Scotty to tell them we should get out of there.

Then the old woman started to mumble. She moved her boney hands up and down quickly. I couldn't understand her. Mellie, Scotty and I looked at each other.

"I'm sorry, we can't under—" I started to say.

Then she spoke loudly. "Evil is here. It's all around you. Darkness will follow wherever you go. Keep your mind clear to help those you hold dear."

Then she reached for us.

I knew we should have left, I thought.

Scotty was closest to her. Her scrawny, gnarled hand grabbed his shirt. He tried to break free. "Help," he yelped, trying to back away, looking surprised and afraid of how strong she was. She held on tightly, pulling him to her.

Mellie and I grabbed Scotty around the waist and pulled hard. He fell backward into our arms. We all tumbled to the ground. Then a sickeningly sweet smell engulfed us. I could barely breathe because of it. Mellie put her hand over her nose. Scotty pinched his nostrils together. We tried to get up, to get away from that smell. Then we heard the hissing—angry, agitated hissing. We couldn't move. We were frozen in place.

At first, I saw nothing. The next instant, we were surrounded by snakes! Huge, ugly snakes. Their bodies were longer and thicker than normal snakes. Many of them had red jagged scars on their bodies. As big as they were, their heads were even bigger. Some of them had deep gashes on their heads. Most of them were black, but some were putrid green or blood red. When the snakes opened their mouths, they were full of spikey, steel gray teeth. These hideous snakes were on the ground, slithering, staring at us. For just one second, I thought I saw sadness in their eyes. But in the next instant, the sadness was gone. I must have imagined it because now they were smiling evilly at us.

How can snakes smile evilly? I thought.

But I couldn't think about that now. There was something strange about their faces. Their eyes. They didn't look like snake eyes. They were round with different colors in them. Not like any snake eyes I'd ever seen anyway.

We didn't have time to figure out what type of snakes these were. Their long, razor-sharp tongues darted out and tried to reach us. They wanted to taste us! They wanted to eat us!

One snake wrapped itself around Mellie's body. As she tried to break free, it quickly tightened its grip on her, hissing loudly as it did. "It's squeezing me to death!" she screamed.

"Now's a good time to do something, Evil Destroyer!" shouted Scotty.

That got my brain working. I remembered I had the bag of

my magic Stun and Run powder in my pocket. Hoping it would work, I pulled it out. I threw a handful of it at the snake's head.

The serpent made a loud, furious hissing. It shook its head violently and then made a gagging sound. It let go of Mellie. That made it enraged. It tried to spit black poisonous venom at her but missed. The ground where the venom hit smoked with a sickeningly sweet, sizzling, burning smell.

Then the old woman started to scream or laugh. I couldn't tell which. It was high-pitched. "You are warned," she said. "You will be destroyed. Others will die."

Chills ran up and down my spine. Mellie and Scotty were shaking in terror.

Scotty and I grabbed Mellie. We were trying to avoid being bitten by the huge, ugly snakes that were swirling around us. Their heads darted out, getting closer to us. They were getting ready to strike.

The old woman pointed her stick up into the air. A lightning bolt exploded from it and flew into the sky. The whole area around us lit up. The gloves with the green markings we saw in the woods appeared out of nowhere and fell to the ground. We stared at them. Then we looked up.

That's when the old woman's hood fell back, and we saw her face.

We took off running for our lives. The snakes were bad enough, but her face was far worse.

CHAPTER 11

We kept running and running. Trees and bushes were a blur as we sped past them. We kept going until we couldn't take another step. Then we just fell on the grass in front of my house.

I was so scared I was trembling. Mellie and Scotty were in the same shape. We couldn't believe what we had just gone through.

"Did you see her face?" Mellie asked in disgust and terror. She was shaking her head and body, as if she was trying to shake off the entire experience.

"See it? I'll never *unsee* it for as long as I live!" Scotty exclaimed. His eyes were so large and filled with horror that I could almost see the whole scenario playing again across his brain like a movie screen.

"Her face was so scarred and disfigured, it was hard to look at her directly," I said.

Her hair had hung in thin, dirty, white strands around her face. Her nose was just twisted cartilage. Her eyes were lifeless and cloudy gray. Despite the gross and frightening view, the thing that stood out the most were her teeth. They were a mixture of black and yellow and were pointed at the tips. Wet sticky black saliva hung from her mouth.

"That was the ugliest, scariest face I have ever seen," I said. "And she didn't have any lips that I could see."

"No. There were no lips," cried Mellie. "Ugh!"

"I didn't see any lips either," said Scotty, with a look of nausea on his face. "How could she not have lips?"

"Who was she, and where do you think she came from, Ollie?" asked Mellie.

"And what about those snakes? Where did *they* come from?" Scotty could barely get the words out. He looked like he was going to throw up.

"I don't know, but that sickeningly sweet stench was what I smelled before, in the dark gray smoke. I'm sure they are a part of whatever is going on here."

"I've never seen her before," said Mellie.

"Oh, we would have remembered her. And we've never seen snakes like that here before either," said Scotty as he cleaned his glasses.

"What was she doing here?" asked Mellie.

"I don't know," I said. "She was telling us something, but I'm not sure what."

"Maybe it was to leave her alone or leave that area of the woods," Scotty suggested. "I would be happy to leave her alone." He wiped sweat from his eyes.

"It could be," I said. "But I think there's more to it." I was trying to make sense of the whole thing. "Let's go over what she said. I think she might be the evil Serpent Witch from the legend."

At first, we couldn't remember her words, just that we were so frightened. We couldn't put our thoughts together. We were just relieved to have gotten away from her.

After a while, we started to calm down. We sat on the grass. We got away. We were safe. We were able to think a little more clearly. What that ugly, old witch said was slowly coming back to us.

I started to remember. "She said, 'You are warned. You will be destroyed. Others will die.'"

"It was a threat," said Scotty. "She wanted to kill us."

"Yes," said Mellie, quickly nodding.

"She also said, 'Evil is here,'" I continued. "'It's all around you. Darkness will follow wherever you go.'"

"She was telling us we would never get away," cried Scotty as he took off his glasses. His hands were shaking. This was getting to be too much for him... for all of us.

?TER 12

> [handwritten note in left margin:] The first book in the Scary Shivers mysteries is still available. The author says the book following this one will be out in 2023. Go to ScaryShivers.com for all information.

o the woods. I didn't tell Mellie or
hey needed a break from this
was happening. I needed to think

solving this mystery was in the
g something? Why the woods?
l, I thought.
m these woods. We saw the ugly,
it possible that she had returned
If that were the case, we needed
to stop this… NOW!

What should we do? It all seems impossible! As I entered the woods, thoughts were swirling around in my head over and over. I had a lot of questions. I didn't have any answers.

It was early afternoon when I found a spot near a small creek and sat down on the grass. I noticed the wind was picking up. Leaves and twigs flew around me. Something hit my foot.

I absently rubbed the spot. I glanced down to see what had hit me. It was a small brown box.

What is this? I picked it up. The box was old and worn. It looked like it had writing on it. It was not easy to read. The words were scratched deep into the wood. Dirt was wedged in the words. It seemed like some kind of warning.

That can't be right, I thought. All that had happened was affecting how I saw everything. I saw or heard warnings everywhere. *Just take it easy*, I thought.

I scrutinized it closely. Sure enough, on the top of the box there were words. I could barely make them out. It read, "Do not open if you value your life!"

Of course, it would say that, I thought. That was fine with me.

I put it down.

I picked it up.

I couldn't explain why I couldn't leave it alone and walk away. I turned it all around and shook it. I thought I heard something. It sounded like a murmur. I shook it again. Nothing. Just an old box, I thought and threw it to the ground. I went to kick it away, but something stopped me. Just a feeling I had.

I shook my head and picked it up. I set it on a rock and stared at it.

I picked it up again. As I touched the latch of the box, I thought of the warning. I shook my head, thinking that it was just an old box. I tried to open it.

It was locked.

I put it in my pocket.

I swear I felt it moving in my pocket. *It can't be*, I thought.

I ran home and called Mellie and Scotty to come over. They did. Quickly. We went down to my workroom.

The Legend of the Serpent Witch

"Now what?" asked Scotty, with anticipation. I'm sure he was hoping that something good happened.

"Did you come up with any answers?" Mellie asked optimistically.

I showed them the box.

"What is it?" asked Mellie.

"Where did it come from?" asked Scotty.

"I don't know. I found it in the woods," I replied.

"The woods where the strange things are happening?" asked Scotty, gulping noisily. He touched his throat with a quivering hand. He had a worried expression on his face.

"I'm afraid so," I said.

Mellie picked up the box. "It looks old," she said as she examined it. "What's this? There's writing on it. I can barely make it out, but I think it says, 'Do not open if you value your life!'" She quickly put it on the table.

Scotty examined the box like he was expecting it to bite him. "Maybe we should just throw it out," he suggested hopefully.

Scotty turned to Mellie and me and asked, "What did you say?"

We both looked at him questioningly.

"I didn't say anything," I said.

"I didn't either," said Mellie.

"I thought I heard something," Scotty said.

He looked at us and then at the box. A muffled noise was coming from the box.

All three of us surrounded the table and leaned forward,

staring at the box.

"The box is locked, but we could break it open," I suggested.

Mellie nodded in agreement.

"I don't think that's a good idea," said Scotty with a frown.

I picked up the box, intending to break open the lid.

But as soon as I touched the latch, the lid flew open!

We all stepped back in surprise.

"I thought you said it was locked," sputtered Scotty.

"It *was* locked," I insisted.

"It's not locked now," Scotty said with a nervous laugh. His eyes darting back and forth as if trying to find a place to hide if necessary.

"Let's see if anything is inside it," I said.

"I knew you were going to say that," said Scotty.

I glanced at Mellie and Scotty, then the box, and then we took a step forward. Even Scotty.

As we did, green smoke flew out of the box and swirled into the air.

We all stumbled backward. Scotty lost his balance. Mellie grabbed him to prevent him from falling.

We stared in astonishment and shock at what happened next. The green smoke materialized into a boy—a boy from another age!

CHAPTER 13

We stared in wonder. We couldn't believe our eyes! Scotty took his glasses off and actually rubbed his eyes.

The boy was about our age. His clothes were different than ours, though. He wore black pants, a tattered brown shirt, and a rope for a belt. His feet were bare. He had nothing on his head.

We turned to run out of my workroom.

Then the boy smiled at us.

We stopped in our tracks. "Are you real?" whispered Scotty.

"Where did you come from?" asked Mellie.

"Who are you?" I asked.

The boy seemed to be examining us and the surroundings. Just when it appeared he wasn't going to say anything, he whispered, "Thank you."

We had to lean forward to hear him.

"I have been in there for a very long, long time," he said.

The boy stared at us. We stared at him. There was only silence.

"You're welcome," I said finally. I didn't know what else to say. I still couldn't believe he was standing there. A boy doesn't materialize out of a small box every day.

"Who are you?" I asked again.

"Are you a ghost?" asked Scotty.

"Where did you come from?" asked Mellie.

"My name is Adrian. I am not a ghost," he said with a smile. "I was put in this box by an evil Serpent Witch."

When we heard "evil Serpent Witch," Mellie, Scotty, and I froze.

"I see. You have heard of her," Adrian said with a knowing expression.

"We have heard of a legend of a Serpent Witch," I said. "She may be here in our town. However, we thought she was just a myth. She couldn't have done all the horrible things the legend claimed she did and be real."

Adrian shook his head sadly. "Unfortunately, she was real and did do horrible things, especially to children. Her name was Hagatha."

CHAPTER 14

"I was her apprentice," said Adrian. "I did many duties for her. Gathered her herbs, mixed her potions, and made sure everything was to her liking. She was old and ugly, but I didn't know she was evil. She hid that well from me. Until one evening when she thought I was away."

Mellie, Scotty and I listened intently.

Adrian continued. "I had left for the night to help a village family gather wheat for the winter. One of their children was ill. I told them I had some herbs that might ease the child's illness. I went back to the hut and discovered the witch's awful secret." Adrian shook his head as if trying to dispel the thought. "Hagatha had convinced two children to come into her hut. She probably said she would give them something they liked. The children knew they shouldn't go with her, but she seemed nice. Their lives were difficult, and if she had something good for them, they thought they would be careful and go with her. If something happened, they would just run away."

Mellie was shaking her head and Scotty was fidgeting with his glasses, as we all realized what Adrian was telling us.

The Legend of the Serpent Witch

"Once they followed her into her hut, she tricked them into her secret room," Adrian continued. "She said she had some sweetmeats and honey for them. Once they were in there, she filled bowls of sweetmeats and honey for them. When they weren't looking, she mixed a special potion into their meal. They soon started to feel drowsy. A few minutes later, the children woke up, but they couldn't move or talk. They were paralyzed."

Mellie, Scotty and I looked at Adrian in horror.

"That's not the worst of it," Adrian stopped talking, took a deep breath, and continued. "They watched as she said a special incantation and sprinkled an evil mixture onto them. Within minutes, the children's beauty and goodness turned into white smoke. She quickly captured the smoke in jars.

"She went to the cupboard door and opened it. Then she turned to them and smiled. She said, 'Now my pets would like to meet you.'

"The children watched in horror as she released her pet snakes upon them. She let her snakes eat and devour their bodies. The children tasted sweet and were a great treat for her snakes."

"Oh no," Mellie gasped. Scotty turned away, looking at the ground. I just sat there shaking my head no. None of us could believe what we were hearing.

Adrian had a faraway look in his eyes. He shuddered at the memory and wiped a tear from his eye.

After a few moments, he continued, "Later, after her pets were full, Hagatha breathed in the white smoke. Magically, she changed from an ugly old woman to a beautiful young maiden within minutes. I wouldn't have believed it if I hadn't seen it myself.

"Unfortunately, she caught me watching her. I thought I was done for. I turned to run, but she grabbed me. She said nothing would happen to me as long as I continued to help her. I was so scared and horrified that I didn't know what to do. I just nodded, appearing to agree with what she said. I understood that she needed me. That's why she didn't destroy me at that time. I was shocked by what happened. No one knew her secret except me.

"I wanted to tell the village elders what I knew. She must have sensed I was going to reveal her secret. She said she would kill more children if I told anyone. Their deaths would be on my head. She had that hold over me. I didn't want anything to happen to any more children. I was sure, eventually, that she was going to kill me. I knew I had to do something.

"I decided to escape. I gathered a few berries and some apples to take with me, placed them in a bag, and buried them behind the hut. I waited for an opportunity. A few days later, in the dead of night, when all was quiet, I gathered up my meager belongings. I listened intently for any sounds of movement. I heard nothing. I waited a few more minutes. Nothing. I gathered my courage and stepped inch by inch to the hut door. I didn't realize I was holding my breath until I was outside and had to breathe.

"I listened again. Nothing. The moon was full that night, so I could easily see my way. I found the spot where I buried my berries and apples. I started to dig. I didn't see them. I moved over a little, thinking I must be in the wrong spot. I kept digging. After a few minutes, I felt something. 'Finally,' I thought. I wanted to get away from that evil witch as soon as possible.

"I reached into the hole to pull out my food. But what I pulled out wasn't my food. It was the head of a large dead snake with its tongue sticking out. I yelled out in revulsion as I dropped the head. Suddenly, a dark shadow covered the hole. I didn't want to turn around. I knew who it was. The air had stilled. There wasn't a sound except my breathing.

"'Going somewhere?' Hagatha whispered. Her face was a mask of evil. To my surprise, she laughed delightedly.

"'I couldn't let you go away just like that. If you want to leave so badly, I know a better way,' she told me. That scared me more than anything. That's when I realized she knew what I was going to do. She already had a plan to get rid of me. I shook with fear.

"Causing pain and suffering gave her great pleasure. She thought I would suffer more if she put a curse on me. She said, 'Let's see if the children you care so much about care as much about you.'

"I can still hear her high-pitched wild laughter. She was happy with herself. She thought she had devised the perfect punishment for me. 'I will put a curse on you, Adrian, and imprison you in this little box. The only one who can unlock this box is a child with goodness in their heart and no fear for their own safety. Good luck in finding that! Because if you don't, you will be imprisoned for all eternity.' She then laughed that scary laugh of hers, and I was instantly confined inside the small box. I have been there ever since."

Mellie and Scotty looked at me. I don't think they believed the 'goodness in their heart' explanation would pertain to me. I shrugged.

Adrian shook his head sadly. "My poor mother, Zara, probably never knew what became of me. When I discovered what Hagatha was doing, I didn't want to tell her what I discovered because I was afraid she might confront Hagatha. I didn't want to put my mother in danger. I have been in here for centuries, until now. You released me," he said with great appreciation and relief.

"You're finally free now," I said.

"Just for a few minutes," Adrian said regrettably.

"What do you mean?" asked Mellie.

"I can't break the curse," Adrian said dejectedly. "For me to be permanently released, Hagatha must be destroyed. I need help from someone with immense goodness in his heart to do this. Then the curse can be broken. However, it is a very dangerous task to fulfill."

"We have a problem, too," I said. "I think we may be able to help each other. Solving our problem will help to release you."

Adrian looked at us doubtfully. "What is your problem?"

"Several children have gone missing over the years," I said. "No one knows what happened to them. Now two more children are missing. We found some items in the woods—kids' clothes, a scarf, a hat, some gloves. When we returned, the items weren't there. We came back another time, and they were back again. It's a mystery. We can't explain it. We heard about the legend of the Serpent Witch, but we didn't really believe it."

Adrian nodded in understanding. "It is hard to believe. But it is true," he said. "She did exist, and it seems she still does exist. She takes children, and they are never seen again. She leaves some of their belongings to draw other children in. This way, she knows where they will be."

I nodded. "As I said, we didn't really believe the legend of the Serpent Witch. Then something happened in the woods that made us believers. She appeared before us. At first, we didn't know what to do. Then, somehow, the gloves we found in the woods fell to the ground. She started to chant something. We didn't know what it meant. Then we saw her face. It was horrible." I was talking fast, unsure if I was making sense or not.

Adrian took it all in. "It could be Hagatha, or it could be her accomplice. She needs someone to assist her so she can remain undetected. Beware," he warned.

A troubled expression crossed his face. "The curse is pulling me back into the box." He said quickly, "Now that you have released me, I can appear if you need my assistance. But my time outside the box is limited. Put your hand on your heart, then tap the box three times. Then repeat 'Free Adrian' three times." His voice started to fade, and we could barely see him. "You must stop her, or more children will disappear, never to be seen again!"

"But how?" I asked. I was too late.

Green smoke surrounded Adrian. It disappeared back into the box. He was gone.

CHAPTER 15

I knew now that the legend was true. The Serpent Witch was taking children. Maybe I could find her lair. I was scared, but I felt very sad for Adrian and the missing children. After Adrian disappeared into the box, I kept it in my pocket. I absently rubbed my pocket. Feeling determined, I gathered my courage. I knew I had to help him.

I told Mellie and Scotty I was going to find the Serpent Witch. At first, they just stared at me like I was crazy. Then, they shared a knowing glance, communicating silently.

Mellie put her fist out and said, "Friends Forever."

Scotty followed her example.

We bumped fists. "Friends Forever," I said, smiling.

Soon after that Mellie, Scotty, and I made our way back to the woods. I had my flashlight in case it started to get dark before we left. Hopefully, we would be long gone before then.

We went to where we had found the hat, scarf, and gloves. We couldn't find anything this time.

"Nothing here," Scotty said, relieved.

"Once again, everything appears normal," said Mellie.

"Yes, too normal," I said, gazing around suspiciously.

Suddenly, we felt a disturbance in the air. The wind swirled around us. The leaves on the trees trembled and fell to the ground around our shoes, trying to scurry away from what was coming. They disappeared quickly. I wanted to scurry away quickly, too, but I didn't. I could tell Mellie and Scotty wanted to be anywhere but here. I smiled to give them encouragement. I didn't think it worked, but at least they stayed with me.

We could hear the sound of moaning in the wind.

I couldn't tell which direction it was coming from. Mellie and Scotty looked around frantically and then at me.

"It sounds like it's all around us," gulped Scotty.

Goose bumps rose on my arms. Mellie must have been feeling them, too. She was rubbing her arms. Scotty couldn't stand still.

Something scurried across a path down in front of us. Our heads turned in unison to see what it was. We didn't see anything except the woods.

"We should go check that out," I said, not really wanting to do that.

"That isn't the best idea you ever had," Scotty said. His eyes were so large they were bigger than his glasses. He could barely stay in place.

"I agree with Scotty. We should come back another day," suggested Mellie.

"Something is trying to scare us away. We don't scare that easily. Right?" I asked expecting them to agree with me. Sort of anyway.

The Legend of the Serpent Witch

They didn't say anything. They just stared at me.

"Well, do we?" I repeated.

"Maybe you don't," said Scotty, as he started to sneak off in the opposite direction.

"Oh, no you don't." Mellie grabbed Scotty's arm and pulled him back. "We stay together."

"Let's keep looking. If you're stuck, keep moving forward," I said and proceeded ahead.

"There he goes again with that forward business. Maybe we... ow!" cried Scotty, rubbing his arm. Mellie had just pinched it.

"We stay together," repeated Mellie firmly.

Scotty made a face and stuck his tongue out at her as we headed deeper into the woods.

CHAPTER 16

We left the path and were walking deeper in the woods. We came across an old rundown hut. "I've never seen this before," I said.

"I haven't either, but it's not surprising that it's here," said Mellie. "It could have been used by hunters at some time."

"I've never noticed it before, and I don't want to notice it now," said Scotty.

We went inside. First me, then Scotty, who was almost being pushed in by Mellie. It was very dark. We couldn't see anything. I was glad I had brought my flashlight with me. I pulled it out and turned it on. After a few minutes, our eyes began to adjust.

Cobwebs were everywhere.

"Yuk," said Mellie as she tried to pull them out of her hair.

"You can say that again," said Scotty as he tried to clean them from his glasses. They stuck to his fingers and then his clothes as he tried to wipe them off.

Many spiders and other creepy crawlers scrambled around. Everything was very quiet except for the scurrying noises they made as they tried to get away from my light.

"Good," I said. "Run, run, run away. Come back another day... when we're not here!"

All of a sudden, we heard high-pitched laughing. I couldn't tell if it was in front of us or behind us. It seemed to be all around us.

I stopped abruptly. Mellie and Scotty bumped into me.

"We should get out of here," whispered Scotty.

"I'm with Scotty," Mellie whispered back.

"What about you, Ollie?" asked Scotty nervously, touching his glasses.

There was no answer.

"Ollie?" Mellie whispered more loudly.

The high-pitched laughter grew louder.

"Ollie?" squeaked Scotty.

I yelled out, "Let go of me." Then I stepped out of the shadows.

Mellie and Scotty both screamed.

"It's OK. It's OK. It's me," I said. "Someone grabbed me. It was a boney hand. Then it let me go. It all happened so quickly I didn't have a chance to yell out." There was a red handprint on my arm.

"Who grabbed you?" asked Mellie as she touched my arm.

"*Why* did they grab you?" asked Scotty, anxiously looking around.

"I'm not sure," I said. Sweat was gathering on my forehead from fear. "Let's find out."

"Who are you?" I asked whoever or whatever was there. My voice was quivering.

Suddenly, a voice said, "You must hurry away. You are all in danger. Evil is here. Evil is there. Find the secret if you dare. What is light is dark. What is dark is light. Evil lurks everywhere."

Oh no, I thought. *Not again.* It was the voice of the ugly, old witch.

"Let's get out of here," I yelled.

Mellie and Scotty were already running ahead of me.

When I thought that we couldn't run anymore, I said, "I think we're safe for right now." We stopped. We were still in the forest, near the area where we found the cap and scarf.

Mellie bent over, trying to catch her breath. Scotty leaned against a tree to steady himself. It was an odd-looking tree, like two trees had grown together. It didn't seem quite right. He was breathing hard. So was I.

"That was creepy," I said.

"I know. But was she warning us or trying to trick us somehow?" asked Mellie.

"I don't know," I said, confused. "She grabbed me. I thought she was going to take me away and hurt me. But then it sounded like she was warning us. I'm just not sure what to think."

Scotty was unusually quiet.

"What do you think, Scotty?" asked Mellie

There was no answer.

Scotty was gone!

CHAPTER 17

We searched everywhere. We started where we had seen him last, by the odd-looking tree. Then we expanded our search, widening the area.

We didn't know what to do. Mellie kept yelling out, "Scotty, Scotty," her voice getting shriller and more panicked with each yell. But there was no answer. Our friend had just disappeared.

We searched for Scotty for about an hour, with no luck. Discouraged, we finally stopped. We couldn't believe it. We couldn't find Scotty! How was that possible?

Mellie said anxiously, "Where is he? We have to find him. We have to find him *now*, Ollie."

Mellie looked so scared. I tried not to show how scared I was, too. Trying to sound encouraging, I said, "I don't know. We need help. There is only one person who may be able to help us."

"Who?" asked Mellie hopefully.

"Aggie," I said. "She said she was concerned about the missing kids because they had been in her shop. She said if there was any way she could help, she would. Maybe she'll help us."

"Yes, you're right," Mellie said, clearly relieved at the thought of someone helping us.

We ran to the candy shop to tell Aggie what had happened and enlist her aid.

We went inside, but Aggie wasn't there. No one was around at all.

"She must be in the back, getting a delivery," I said.

"Yes, that must be it," said Mellie. She was pacing back and forth, impatiently waiting for Aggie to come out.

We peered out the window, hoping that we might see Scotty somehow. No chance of that, though.

We waited, getting more and more worried about Scotty. Then I saw that the office door, which was usually locked, was ajar.

Maybe Aggie was in there and hadn't heard us come in. I looked in the office. Unfortunately, Aggie wasn't there. Then something caught my eye. I went into the office to check it out. Mellie followed me in.

There was a large bookshelf, with several shelves, displaying dozens of items from different cities. Some had the name of the city or attraction on them. Aggie had said she moved around a lot.

One item in particular caught my attention. It looked like an autographed baseball. But it didn't seem quite right. It was like someone, a child, just wrote his name on the ball, as if to identify it as his. Very odd. Johnny Knapp. *Who's that?* I wondered. *Sounds familiar.* I picked it up to examine it more closely when the bookshelf slid sideways, exposing a secret room.

I jumped back. *What is this?* I thought. *Why would she have a secret room? To hide valuable stuff?* I couldn't believe what I saw inside. I quickly scanned the room. My eyes were seeing something unthinkable. My brain hadn't caught up yet to what it all meant. My mind was racing. It was clicking on events from the past to the present. *Oh no, it can't be…*

That's when someone grabbed my arm.

CHAPTER 18

It was Mellie.

"We should get out of here," she said nervously as she pulled on my arm.

"Mellie, look at all of this." The tone of my voice must have caught her attention.

Mellie apprehensively gazed around, farther into the secret room.

"Come on," I said. I took her hand and we entered the room.

Toys, bits of clothing, jewelry, shoes, hats, scarves, among other things were everywhere. Hundreds of them. Some were on shelves. Others were on tables. Many of them were on the floor in piles. Some appeared to be very old, from centuries ago.

"What are these?" asked Mellie not really understanding what she was seeing. She frowned. The more she examined the items in the room, the more worried she seemed. "Ollie…" she said.

I nodded my understanding.

She picked up a scarf. The same one we saw in the woods. "Ollie, this is the same scarf we found." She handed me the scarf. "Why would Aggie…" Her eyes widened with disbelief. The truth and horror dawned on her quickly.

"I know," I said, breathing deeply, trying to stay calm. "Aggie must be the Serpent Witch!"

We stared at each other, hoping that if we didn't move, it might all disappear. That it might not be real. But it was real. It was right in front of us.

I collected my thoughts and tried to make sense of all this. "She destroyed children and took their youth and goodness," I said. "She stayed young. She moved around a lot. That's how she stayed undetected all this time."

We were lost in our thoughts when the door creaked. We slowly turned towards the door, afraid of what we'd see. Our nerves were on edge.

Then, from behind us, came a voice…

We jumped, knocking into each other.

"Welcome *Evil Destroyer*. I see you've found out my little secret," Aggie said, laughing. We turned around quickly. Aggie stood there, smiling, an evil and satisfied gleam in her eye.

Delighted by the alarm on our faces.

CHAPTER 19

We didn't know, at the time, that Scotty had fallen or was pulled into the odd-looking tree. He hit his head on one of the walls as he fell. He got up and shook his head, trying to clear it.

"Where am I?" Scotty asked. "What just happened?"

He couldn't see anything except a light in the distance.

Where are Ollie and Mellie? Scotty thought. *They were just with me. The last thing I remember is leaning against the tree, and now, here I am.* He pushed on the walls, trying to find a way out. But nothing happened. He yelled, "Ollie? Mellie? Where are you?" But there was only silence.

As he was trying to figure out what to do, he slowly became aware of something that made his blood freeze in his veins. It was that sickeningly sweet smell again. There was no mistaking it. *Oh no*, he thought. *This time they're going to get me, for sure. No one will know what happened to me.*

I'm all alone here. I've got to get out of here. He started toward the light. "Ollie, Mellie," he whispered with every step.

Suddenly, Scotty felt a presence behind him. He was hoping that it was Mellie or Ollie. Before he could call out, a hand covered his mouth, and he was being dragged away backward. He struggled, but it was no use; the person was too strong. A cloth bag was placed over his head.

Somehow, I have to get free and help my friends, he thought. His heart was beating fast, and he couldn't breathe well with the bag over his face. *Now, what am I going to do?* he thought. *I'm doomed for sure.* Tears ran down his face. His last thoughts were, *Friends forever.* He tried to fist bump but couldn't. Then all went black.

Scotty woke up slowly. He shook his head to clear it. *At least I'm not dead,* he thought, relieved. *Or am I?* He wasn't sure yet.

He looked around to see where he was. It was dark and spooky. He tried to get up but found a metal ring around his wrist was attached to a chain. The chain was attached to the wall. It was long enough for him to move around just a bit, but not much.

Well, I'm not dead. Dead people don't get chained to the wall. Maybe I'm dreaming, he thought hopefully. In one way, he was relieved. He couldn't get hurt if he was dreaming. But he knew he wasn't.

Now what? He was scared. He tried to pull on the chain to dislodge it from the wall. It wouldn't budge. He tried again with all his might. Still nothing. He kept trying until his arm hurt so much, he had to stop.

Now I've had it, he thought. *The Serpent Witch has me.* Just the thought that he was in the hands of the evil witch made him start yelling for Ollie and Mellie. He yelled and yelled. There was no answer. Only silence and the beating of his heart. He started to scream again but stopped.

He thought he heard something. He wasn't sure what it was. He listened closely, afraid to breathe. There it was again. It sounded like a door creaking. It wasn't far from him. He couldn't see anything but darkness. Pitch-black darkness. Then he heard footsteps.

His heart skipped a beat. He wasn't sure if he was happy or scared. The footsteps were coming closer. And closer…

He peered into the darkness. Nothing. Then Scotty heard a voice. He wasn't sure who it was. His heart beat faster and faster. He tried frantically to pull on the chain.

Oh no, he thought, *I'm done for now. All hope for escape is gone. My parents will be so mad at me if I disappear,* he worried. Then someone turned on a light.

"Good, good, I see I still have you. That is very fortunate," she said.

"You!" Scotty shouted, surprised and confused.

It was the librarian, Cassandra!

CHAPTER 20

Back at the candy shop, Mellie and I were shocked by our discovery.

"Aggie!" I exclaimed.

"But it can't be," said Mellie in disbelief.

Aggie laughed once more. "But it is," she said with glee. "I fooled you like I fooled all the others. I always get what I want."

"But we don't understand," said Mellie.

"We thought you were the only one who would listen to us and help us," I said.

"Of course, you did," Aggie said. "Children are always so gullible. That is how I've been so successful and undetected all these centuries." She chuckled happily at her own brilliance.

"I thought I was safe here for a while longer. Then you kids started poking around." She angrily pointed at Mellie and me. "I guess it doesn't really matter. I'll get what I want here. I always do. And I'll get it from you." She leered at us in a way that made my skin crawl.

"We haven't done anything to you," I said indignantly.

Mellie shook her head in agreement.

"It doesn't matter. I swore revenge against the people in my village who were mean to me and made fun of me centuries ago. I tricked their children into thinking I had something good for them. Children are very useful to me. I was ugly, and their youth and goodness made me beautiful and young. I enjoyed it. I craved it. I need it to live. I feel like I'm getting my revenge over and over again. It's wonderful!" Aggie seemed very proud of herself. She cackled wildly.

"I'll take care of you two, now that you know my secret. I was only going to kill Scotty…"

Mellie and I looked at each other nervously.

Aggie shrugged as if it wasn't really a concern. "More for me and my hungry pet snakes," she said with a wicked smile. "I will act like I am concerned about your disappearance, then one day, I will be gone."

"What are you going to do with us?" I asked. I didn't really want to know.

"Because of your meddling, I have to move on before I planned. For you, I have something special in mind." When she saw the horror on our faces, she started giggling with an evil gleam in her eye. She stepped toward us, reaching out.

CHAPTER 21

Scotty couldn't believe his eyes. "Cassandra!?! You... you're the Serpent Witch!" he exclaimed. "But we liked you."

She laughed at his confusion. "You're not too smart, are you? You will see," she said happily.

"What will you do with me?" he asked, afraid of what she might say.

"You will see," she repeated, not willing to tell him anything else.

"When?" he pushed for an answer. "My friends will be looking for me. You'd better let me go." He hoped that would upset her.

"My friends, my friends," she mimicked him and laughed. "Your friends have their own problems."

With no more explanation, Cassandra turned off the light and left him chained to the wall in complete darkness.

I have to help Ollie and Mellie, he thought. He pulled on the chain. *But how?*

CHAPTER 22

As Aggie reached for us, Mellie backed into me. I tried to push her behind me. We shrank back...

Aggie grabbed us and dragged us toward the back storeroom. I tried fighting her off, but she was surprisingly strong. She pushed us into the room. We stumbled in, falling to the ground.

"Oh, Oliver," Mellie said. "What are we going to do?" I could tell she was trying not to cry. I was trying not to cry, too. I rubbed my eyes to stop the tears from coming out.

Before leaving, Aggie said, "I'll be back soon to take care of the two of you. You won't like what I have in store for you, but it will give me great pleasure. Here," she threw in a bottle of water. "This should keep you going until I get back. Enjoy it. It will be the *last* thing you ever taste." She beamed with anticipation.

Then Aggie left, slamming the door shut behind her. We could hear her evil snickers echo down the hall.

I quickly ran to the door to check if it was locked. I turned the handle, holding my breath. It was locked. *Oh well, I had to try.*

"What did she mean about only killing Scotty?" Mellie asked. "I can't even think about Scotty being in danger."

"I don't know what she meant," I said. "Somehow, she got a hold of Scotty. That's when he disappeared." I thought back to when we couldn't find him. "I can't think about Scotty being in danger, either. We have to help Scotty and ourselves before it's too late."

"I know, but how?" she asked, her voice quivering. She kept wringing her hands.

I paced back and forth, trying to find a solution. I put my hand down accidentally and touched my pants pocket. Something was sticking out.

Then it dawned on me. "Adrian!" I exclaimed. I felt a glimmer of hope run through me. *Why didn't I think about him before?* I thought. *Of course, if anyone can help us, he can!*

"Oh, Ollie, I was so scared with everything going on, I forgot about Adrian. Yes... maybe he can help us," Mellie said eagerly

I pulled the box out of my pocket where I'd kept it since we found it. I was afraid something might happen to it, and I didn't want to take the chance of losing it.

I put my hand on my heart then tapped the box three times. Then I said the words, "Free Adrian. Free Adrian. Free Adrian." I didn't know if this was some type of magical ritual, but if it worked, it was magic to me.

Nothing happened. The box sat silently in my hand.

"Oh no, Oliver, you must have done it wrong," Mellie said

with a frown. Her eyes were full of apprehension. "Did you do it the way Adrian told you to?"

I glanced at her then at the box. "Maybe I need to…" I started to say and scratched my head, feeling confused. But I never finished my sentence.

Suddenly, the lid flew open, and green smoke swirled into the air. We stared at it in wonder and anticipation.

Swiftly, Adrian appeared before us. We quickly stepped toward him. We weren't afraid anymore.

"We need your help!" I said in a rush.

"I know," he said sadly, shaking his head.

"The witch has Scotty! We have to help him," Mellie said fearfully.

I explained all that happened. I told Adrian about finding the hut and something grabbing me. About the voice warning us. About being scared and running away. And then discovering Scotty was gone.

Adrian listened carefully and took it all in. His expression was sorrowful when I spoke of Scotty and not knowing where he was.

I told him about going to Aggie for help. About finding the secret room and all the items belonging to missing children. Our shock in finding out that Aggie was indeed the Serpent Witch.

"So, Hagatha calls herself Aggie now," Adrian said, nodding in understanding.

"Adrian, please help us," I pleaded. "We must find Scotty and destroy the evil witch."

The Legend of the Serpent Witch

"I'll do whatever I can to help you. I only hope that it's not too late," said Adrian.

CHAPTER 23

Scotty felt a renewed determination come over him after Cassandra left. *I need to get out of here*, he thought. *She can't hold me here*. Thinking about helping Ollie and Mellie was all he could focus on. He struggled with the chain, but it still wouldn't budge.

Scotty tried to squeeze his hand through the metal ring around his wrist, but it wouldn't fit through. He even tried spitting on his wrist, hoping that would make it slippery enough to slide through.

"Yuck, and it didn't even work," he said shaking his head. He tried pulling his wrist through the metal ring so many times that it began to bleed. He couldn't see it, but felt the blood dripping down his wrist. But he wasn't ready to give up yet.

He pulled and pulled the chain attached to the wall, but it didn't move at all. *There must be some way to get out of here*, he thought.

Scotty kept thinking about what might be happening to Mellie and Ollie. He hoped they were all right. He needed to help them. He would do anything to help them. *I want to see them again*, he thought. He was near tears at the thought of never seeing his friends again.

Not knowing what else to do, he sat on the ground, frustrated and miserable.

Suddenly, Scotty thought he heard a sound. He listened intently. It sounded like scratching.

What is that? he wondered. "I hope it's not rats smelling my blood," he said out loud.

Oh no, they're going to eat my arm off, Scotty thought as he frantically pulled on the chain.

Then the noise changed. The scratching turned into a clicking.

Maybe it's Ollie and Mellie, he hoped. He listened closely, then Scotty heard a grumbling. *This can't be good*, he thought anxiously. *That doesn't sound like them.*

Abruptly, the door to the room flew open. A bright light illuminated the doorway. He fell back against the wall in fear. The light was blinding. Scotty tried blinking to clear his vision. Then he rubbed his eyes. He couldn't believe who he saw in the doorway.

"Oh no," he groaned.

Just when he thought it couldn't get any worse…in stepped the ugly, old, witch.

So, Cassandra isn't the Serpent Witch? Scotty questioned, very confused. *Cassandra must be her assistant, and this is the Serpent Witch.*

Scotty froze. He didn't know what was going to happen now. He started to silently pray. *Please get me out of this, and I won't be such a chicken anymore…*

The old boney witch was staring right at him. His eyes darted back and forth as he scanned the room trying to figure out how to run away.

I'll be nicer to my parents, he bargained. *Even if sometimes they make me clean my room and I don't want to…*

Then the boney witch spoke loudly. "Nothing is what it seems. Your friends are in jeopardy, and they will not last. Soon they will be in the past."

Scotty was so frightened that he didn't understand what she was trying to say. Speechless, he could only stare at her.

She stepped toward him. Not knowing what she was going to do, Scotty pulled frantically on the chain. He couldn't believe it when she put a key in the lock and undid the chain. He was free! Scotty stared at her. She didn't say anything. Scotty didn't want to stick around waiting to hear what she had to say. As he took his first step to run away, her voice stopped him.

"Come quickly if you want to see your friends again. Alive," she said.

That's all Scotty had to hear. *Why would the Serpent Witch free him?* He didn't know if he could trust her, but he definitely wasn't going to stay here. *If there is a chance to help Mellie and Ollie, I have to take it,* he thought. He followed the ugly, old witch out of the room. They left the building and went into the night.

Scotty looked up to the stars. "Thank you for answering my prayers. Please let my friends be OK," he whispered, taking his glasses off for a moment. He swiped a hand across his face, wiping away tears.

The Legend of the Serpent Witch

Later, Cassandra returned to get Scotty. She saw the chain dangling from the wall and Scotty was nowhere to be seen. She looked everywhere. She couldn't find him. He was gone.

"How did he... Oh no, Hagatha isn't going to like this," Cassandra said nervously. "This isn't going to go well —for any of us," she added.

CHAPTER 24

Adrian, Mellie and I were still in the back storeroom of the candy shop where Aggie put us. "It will soon be too late for your friend," cautioned Adrian.

"Oh no," said Mellie, with fear in her voice.

"It can't be," I said. "We must find a way to help him."

"We will try, but first, we have to get you out of here before Hagatha returns," warned Adrian. He started examining the entire room.

"What are you searching for?" I asked.

"Hagatha always had a secret passage in the past," said Adrian. "It would help her have access to children. It might be a hidden door or opening. It must be in here somewhere. Check the walls and floor carefully."

"Mellie, you start on the left side of the room, and I'll check the right side," I said. "We don't have a moment to spare."

Mellie nodded and began to search. Adrian was already checking the floor for any hidden openings.

Mellie and I worked quickly but carefully to find a way out.

We searched and searched. I thought I found something a

couple of times, but it turned out to be nothing that would help us. Mellie couldn't find anything either. We were struggling not to get discouraged.

"Is there nothing here that can help us?" Mellie asked, a bit of panic in her voice. "Is there no way out of here?"

Mellie looked like she was about to cry. She grabbed the bottle of water Aggie left for us and took a sip. As she started to ask me if I wanted a drink, she accidentally dropped the bottle on the floor. I quickly went to retrieve it in case we needed the water. We didn't know how long we would be in this room.

"Look," said Adrian, pointing to the floor.

At first, Mellie and I didn't know what he was pointing at. Then we saw some of the water puddled on the floor near us. The rest had disappeared between the cracks in the floor near the corner of the room.

I bent down to better follow the path of the water. I felt on the tile floor for anything that was out of place or didn't belong there.

"I don't feel anything... wait a minute," I said. "One of these tiles are loose." I was starting to get excited. I tried to pry the loose tile up with my fingertips, but I couldn't quite get a hold of it. I looked around for something to use to pry the tile up. I found a pencil on one of the tables. I grabbed it and stuck the tip of the pencil in the crack next to the tile. But as I tried to lift the tile, the pencil broke.

"Hurry Ollie," said Adrian. "Time is running out."

Mellie spotted a ruler on a shelf. "Here Ollie. Try this," she said.

I took the ruler from Mellie and shoved the corner of it in the crack next to the tile. I pulled on the ruler as hard as I could. Just when I thought the ruler would snap, it lifted the corner of the tile just enough that I could get my fingers under it. I then pulled the tile up and off the floor. "It worked!" I exclaimed.

With one tile out of the way, I was able to remove three more tiles rather easily. With those tiles gone, a metal ring was exposed.

"Look, I think I found a way out…" I pulled on the metal ring. It was attached to a trap door. "There's a trap door here," I said.

"Well done," said Adrian approvingly. "I knew she must have concealed a passage somewhere. Quickly lift the trap door," he instructed. "The sooner we leave here, the better."

I lifted the trap door. I saw nothing but total darkness.

Mellie and I stared at Adrian. I was afraid to go into the darkness. I could tell by the expression on her face Mellie was, too.

"You must go down. Now…" said Adrian, "before it's too late…" His voice was fading.

"Oh no," I said.

The green smoke quickly appeared. It surrounded Adrian. Then Adrian disappeared back into the box.

Mellie and I looked at each other. We weren't staying here, that's for sure.

Down into the darkness, we went.

CHAPTER 25

Mellie and I found ourselves in a narrow tunnel. We had to walk single file in it. It was dark and cold and smelled like rotted meat. I didn't know where it would lead, but it was better than staying up in the room waiting for Aggie to seal our fate.

I pulled out my flashlight. We made our way through the tunnel. It felt like it was descending.

"Where is it leading us?" asked Mellie.

"I don't know," I said. "Hopefully, to Scotty or somewhere we can get help."

"It seems like we keep going down," Mellie said.

"Seems like that to me, too," I said.

Down, down, down, we went. It seemed endless. After a few more minutes, there was a change, and we were going upward. Finally, it felt like the tunnel leveled out.

"It seems like we're just going straight now, Ollie," observed Mellie.

"I think you're right," I said, relief in my voice.

Unexpectedly, we couldn't go any farther. There was a dark wall in front of us.

The Legend of the Serpent Witch

"We're at a dead-end," I said.

"Now what?" asked Mellie, looking around for a way out.

"I'm not sure, but I think there may be some kind of door here," I said. I was checking the wall for any openings. I pushed on the wall.

With just a whisper, the wall opened. We stepped back in surprise. At first, we were afraid to do anything. Then Mellie nodded. I stuck my head out of the door.

With a sigh of relief, I said, "Let's go."

She quickly followed.

We stepped through the doorway to find ourselves in the woods. We had stepped out of a tree… the same odd-looking tree Scotty was leaning against before he went missing!

We were near the place where I had found the scarf and baseball cap. Where we found the gloves was not far from here either.

"Ollie," Mellie said, "I think…"

"You're right, Mellie." I knew what she was going to say. It dawned on me right then, too. "This is how she got the children and how she brought them to her shop undetected."

All of a sudden, from behind us, we heard laughter. Cackling, insane, evil laughter…

CHAPTER 26

To our shock, Aggie was standing a few feet from us.

"Did you really think you could escape me?" she asked incredulously. "No one *ever* escapes me!" She scowled with anger. "*Ever!*" She pointed her finger at us. "You will pay. With your lives, of course," she promised, chuckling.

"Soon, my assistant will be here, and I will take your youth and goodness and destroy you all. Your fate will be a mystery. No one will know what happened to you. Just like all the others," she said confidently.

She put her head back and laughed gleefully.

Then she said with anticipation, "Let us begin…"

She waved her arms in the air and mumbled words we didn't understand. Then, as if by magic, a huge pot took shape in front of us. I peered closely at it. It wasn't a pot at all. It was a cauldron.

Mellie and I could only stare in disbelief. We would have run, but we needed to find out what happened to Scotty. Mellie grabbed my hand. I held on to hers tightly. We tried to give each other courage.

Aggie reached into her pocket. She pulled out two small vials. She opened each vial and emptied the contents slowly, one by one, into the cauldron. One vial had thick black liquid in it. The other vial contained a dark green putrid liquid. Then from another pocket, she pulled out a velvet bag. She scooped out a handful of what looked like dried plants. She mumbled words over them in a language I had never heard before. *"Bulitabai! Bulegalegisa! Bulilevaga!"* She dropped the dried plants into the cauldron as well. The mixture began to bubble and churn. Steam rose from it.

Finally, Aggie put her hand behind her back. I strained to see what she was doing. I didn't have to wait long.

She pulled out three small bottles filled with liquid. The liquid was dark red. I didn't want to know what it was. I could guess, though.

Please don't let that be blood, I said to myself.

"Aah," said Aggie, "the last but most important ingredient—blood."

"Of course, it is," I said to myself. Then I thought, *Whose blood?* I got a sick feeling in the pit of my stomach. *Scotty's? No way. No way.* I wouldn't think about that. *It isn't his.* I changed my mind. I didn't want to know whose blood it was.

Slowly and with relish, Aggie poured the blood into the cauldron. Then she whispered an incantation. The mixture in the cauldron began to rattle and quake. The whole cauldron rumbled. It felt like the ground was beginning to shake with the evil it knew was coming.

In the air came that sickeningly sweet smell. Slowly at first.

Then a little stronger. Then, in the next second, it was all around us, making Mellie and me gag. Then we heard that awful, angry hissing.

Before we knew it, the large, ugly snakes with the strange eyes appeared out of nowhere. They were all around Hagatha. They were agitated. They were spitting black venom and slithering around each other. Their tongues going in and out quickly making a wet slushy sound.

"Be patient, my slithering lovelies," cooed Hagatha. "You will have your treats soon. All in good time. I want to have some fun first." She beamed.

"Oh, Oliver," shuddered Mellie. "What are we going to do?"

"We have to find out what happened to Scotty," I said. I had to believe he was still OK. I couldn't think that he wasn't.

After that, I wasn't sure, but I knew we had to do something. Fast. Or we would never be seen again. And Aggie would be free to do whatever vile and nasty things she wanted to do to other innocent children.

My mind was spinning to find a means of escape. So far, nothing seemed possible. I tried not to let panic overtake my thoughts. I had to think clearly. I considered pulling the box out, but not knowing what happened to Scotty was clouding my mind. *There must be a way out of this*, I thought frantically.

Suddenly, a noise came from behind some trees. It sounded like footsteps. Human footsteps. We all turned toward the trees.

Mellie and I looked at each other encouragingly. I hoped it was someone who could help us. I could tell by her look of anticipation that Mellie felt the same.

At first, I couldn't see who was coming through the trees, as they were very dense. *Whoever it is, I hope they will help us,* I kept thinking.

Footsteps drew closer.

I scanned the woods, hoping help was here. I still couldn't see anyone.

The person was fast approaching.

Before I could yell out for help, Aggie said, "Aah, here comes my assistant now."

"Oh no," I groaned when I saw who it was. All hope left my body in a rush.

Cassandra came into the clearing. Mellie and I were shocked to see that Cassandra was Aggie's assistant. We stood there gaping at Cassandra. I shook my head no in disbelief. When she saw the disbelief on my face, she smiled with delight. Mellie and I squeezed each other's hand tightly and remained silent.

"I was wondering when you'd get here. You're just in time for the fun," Aggie said as she rubbed her hands together and cackled. "Everything is going as planned."

CHAPTER 27

"Well, not everything, exactly," said Cassandra, a perplexed look on her face.

A frightening scowl formed across Hagatha's face. "What do you mean?" she asked sharply.

"I grabbed Scotty and chained him up as you directed," Cassandra explained.

"Yes, it was a simple task. One I thought you could easily handle," said Hagatha with a frown.

"Yes... well... I did handle it... but there seems to be a minor setback," Cassandra said nervously.

"What kind of setback?" Hagatha snapped as she took a step toward Cassandra.

Cassandra backed up in fear. She said nothing.

"Well?" barked Hagatha. "Answer me. What kind of setback? Where *is* Scotty?"

"I chained him up like you said to do…" Cassandra looked at Mellie and me. "He was worried about his friends. He should have been worried about himself. Little did he know what you had in store for him," she said, chuckling, as if trying to lighten up the situation she found herself in.

"And what happened?" Hagatha asked impatiently.

"I'm not sure. Somehow Scotty…" Cassandra paused, unable to look Hagatha in the eye, "got away." Her voice was shaking.

Mellie and I stared at Cassandra, then at each other. We couldn't believe what we had just heard. We didn't even have time to think about it, because Hagatha got our attention.

"What?! You fool! How could you let that happen? He is the last one who could expose us," Hagatha screeched. She took a threatening step toward her.

Cassandra quickly shrank back. "I came to tell you as soon as I found him missing. I will find him…" she pleaded. Cassandra clearly feared for her life.

"You had better," raged Hagatha. "Or…"

The next thing that happened shocked us all.

CHAPTER 28

Scotty bolted into the clearing. Then…

…the ugly, old witched followed him in.

I stared at Scotty. Not really believing it was him and that he was OK. Relief quickly filled my whole body. Mellie had a big smile on her face.

Before I could run to Scotty, I heard a commotion.

"You!" screamed Aggie, pointing to the ugly, old witch. "What are you doing here?"

Mellie and I turned to the old witch. We didn't know what was going on. We thought Aggie was the ugly, old witch.

"I thought I destroyed you centuries ago," said Aggie.

"You thought you did, but you didn't," said the old witch. "I will see you destroyed for what you did in the past. What you did to Adrian."

"I will destroy you first, once and for all. Then I will kill these children!" Aggie screamed madly. She aimed her finger at the ugly, old witch. She seemed determined to finish her.

The old witch moved surprisingly quickly. She dashed behind and past Cassandra to get to the trees. Cassandra darted forward, trying to get out of the way. But she was too late.

Aggie's arm lit up with a flash of light. In an instant a bolt of lightning flew out of her finger and hit Cassandra in the chest. The lightning bolt went right through her.

Cassandra looked down at the hole in her chest in surprise. She lifted her head and gaped at Aggie in confusion. Then she fell to the ground and turned to black dust. The wind swept up her ashes, and she was gone.

Aggie had slaughtered Cassandra. She didn't care. "She was of no use to me anymore," she said.

Scotty, now seeing his chance, ran over to Mellie and me.

Aggie now turned all her attention to us.

CHAPTER 29

Mellie, Scotty and I were alone with Aggie. We needed help. I didn't hesitate. I quickly pulled the box out of my pocket.

I put my hand on my heart then tapped the box three times.

"Free Adrian. Free Adrian. Free Adrian." I couldn't say the words fast enough. With each plea, my voice grew louder and louder, fear making my words move faster than ever out of my mouth.

At first, nothing happened. *Oh no,* I thought. *I'm calling for Adrian too late. We're going to be destroyed.*

Then, miraculously, green smoke flew out of the box and into the air. In a matter of seconds, Adrian appeared before us.

"Adrian!" yelled Aggie in astonishment, pointing her finger at him. "I never thought I would see you again."

"I am happy to say you were wrong, Hagatha," said Adrian. "It is time for your evil ways to end. Now. Many people have suffered and died because of your wickedness."

He stared intently at Mellie, Scotty, and me. Then he said some incantations that I didn't understand. In turn he said to us. "I need your help. Only the strength of your goodness will work here. Each of you must repeat exactly what I say. *Amor et Bonitas Destruet te*," he chanted.

"*Amor et Bonitas Destruet te*," we repeated.

At first, Aggie laughed. "You can't destroy me," she said unconcerned.

We repeated the incantation. "*Amor et Bonitas Destruet te. Amor et Bonitas Destruet te. Amor et Bonitas Destruet te…*"

Then Aggie screamed. She ran toward us and grabbed Scotty by the throat.

He yelled out in fear. "Let go of me." He kept struggling to break free but couldn't. He tried to pry her fingers from his throat. The more he tried, the harder she squeezed. He tried pulling one or two fingers backwards to cause her pain, but she didn't let go. "Ollie, Mellie, help me!" he screamed in terror. His face was turning red, and his eyes were bulging out. She was cutting off his oxygen.

Adrian repeated the chant louder and more forcefully. "Keep repeating it!" he pleaded. We did as he said.

"*Amor et Bonitas Destruet te. Amor et Bonitas Destruet te. Amor et Bonitas Destruet te…*"

Out of the corner of my eye was a flash of movement. Before I had a chance to know what was happening the ugly, old witch suddenly reappeared next to Adrian. I was stunned at how fast she moved. We stared at her. We didn't know what she was going to do. Was she going to help us? I wasn't sure.

"*Amor et Bonitas Destruet te*," she said.

I shook my head. I didn't understand what was going on. I originally thought she was the evil Serpent Witch. She was the one with the gloves with green markings. She kept warning us. I thought she was warning us because she wanted to harm us. When she appeared, the snakes appeared also.

So, why was the ugly, old witch helping Adrian now? Mellie was also staring at her. I could see unanswered questions crossing her face as she watched the old witch.

I couldn't take it all in. I glanced at Scotty. It appeared that he was close to losing consciousness.

Aggie was glaring at Adrian and the old witch with vile hatred in her eyes. She released Scotty. He fell to the ground, holding his throat.

I took a step toward him to help him.

"Keep chanting! Keep chanting!" said Adrian.

Mellie and I did. Scotty did the best he could. The pressure was off his throat and he was able to breathe again. He slowly started to chant along with us.

"No! No! No!" screamed Aggie. "This can't be happening. I will destroy you all."

"We must all hold hands," directed the ugly, old witch. We immediately grabbed each other's hands.

We felt the power of the words "*Amor et Bonitas Destruet te*," increasing with each repetition. I could feel a tingling sensation up and down my arms. It felt electric, like energy. The tingling sensation increased with each repetition.

Aggie shot a look of pure hatred at Adrian and the ugly, old witch. "I won't let this happen," she screeched with spit flying out of her mouth. Aggie took a step toward Adrian and the ugly, old witch. Suddenly, gray smoke appeared from the ground, swirling and surrounding her.

Around and around her, it went. The smoke was getting thicker and swirling faster. Aggie turned her head back and forth as if she couldn't believe her eyes. It was as if she was willing the gray smoke to go away. But it didn't go away. It surrounded her from head to toe.

We stared in astonishment and horror at what happened next.

CHAPTER 30

Aggie's skin turned gray and shriveled. Her young features crumpled away. Her eyes sunk into her face, so far that I could only see cold, lifeless, black pits where her eyes should be. Her nose twisted into an unrecognizable mess. She snarled, her lips were black and cracked, with yellow and green mucous dripping down her crooked chin. She looked so bad that, for a moment, in our shock, our grip lessened. The power of the incantation faded a little.

Aggie wasn't giving up. She wanted revenge one more time. She grabbed Scotty again. But her hand began to turn into a bare bone.

"Oh, no!" Aggie shrieked, a hideous, painful scream. The snakes darted into the whirling gray smoke, as if trying to help Aggie or to get Scotty; we didn't know which.

Then Scotty screamed in terror, "She's taking me with her! Help me!"

We watched in horror. I took a step to help him. But Aggie, the snakes, and Scotty were engulfed in gray smoke that began to turn black. Like death.

We couldn't see any of them.

"Scotty," I yelled in desperation.

Mellie shouted in fear, "We're losing Scotty." Then, with her voice breaking, she said, "Ollie, Scotty is gone."

We had lost our dearest friend.

CHAPTER 31

I couldn't move. How could this have happened? Our dearest friend. Scotty. I should have saved him somehow. I was grief-stricken.

Mellie was crying out loud. Tears of pain and anguish ran down my face. All I could do was stare where Scotty, Aggie, and the snakes had been. I saw nothing but the black smoke.

I was frozen in disbelief. Mellie looked dazed. Tears were wet on her face. She just stood there not blinking. It was as if time had stopped.

How can we go on without Scotty, our friend? I thought.

Adrian and the ugly, old witch were still chanting, louder and faster, over and over, "*Amor et Bonitas Destruet te. Amor et Bonitas Destruet te. AMOR ET BONITAS DESTRUET TE!*"

All of a sudden, there was a crack of thunder, and the smoke cleared. Scotty was lying on the ground. He wasn't moving. I was frozen in place with dread of finding out how he was. We didn't know if he was alive… or not.

CHAPTER 32

Mellie and I ran to Scotty.

He was alive! His breathing was shallow. But he was breathing!

Next to him was a pile of black dust. It was Aggie and the snakes. Or what was left of them.

Scotty was coming to. He smiled up at us. "That was close," he said, hugging Mellie and me.

We helped him to stand. We were crying, laughing, and hugging him all at the same time. "Scotty, Scotty, Scotty," we repeated, not believing he was still alive. We didn't want to let go of him.

We all turned to Adrian and the ugly, old, witch. We couldn't believe what we were seeing.

The ugly, old witch had turned young and beautiful! Her wrinkles disappeared. Her white stringy hair turned to shiny thick black hair. Her nose transformed from twisted cartilage to a small, straight and beautiful nose. Her lifeless, cloudy gray eyes were now vibrant blue. Her mouth with the black and yellow pointed teeth and black saliva, turned into beautiful soft red lips with white teeth. She was looking at Adrian with a stunning smile so bright that the area around us lit up with light.

"Adrian!" she said with her arms out.

"Mother!" said Adrian as he ran into her arms.

"My son…" She kissed and hugged him as if she would never let him go.

Mellie, Scotty, and I hugged each other and cried again. This time with happiness for Adrian and his mother. They were reunited.

The curse was finally over. For both of them. They were safe.

They were happy. They were together.

After a few minutes, Adrian asked, "Mother, how did you…"

"When you disappeared, I knew Hagatha was responsible," Zara explained. "I had doubts about her all along. When I confronted her about what happened to you, she just said you got what you deserved. I couldn't help myself, and I went to attack her. That's when she put a curse on me, declaring that I would be old and ugly throughout the ages. She thought it would be more excruciating for me to live as a decrepit and horrific woman for all eternity —without you—than to kill me."

"But then, how did you find me?" asked Adrian.

Zara took Adrian's hand and continued, "I knew I would always search for you. One day, when Hagatha wasn't around, I sneaked into her hut to look for clues. I found her journal with her writings in it. She wrote about the curse she put on

The Legend of the Serpent Witch

you. And I found the box you were in. I quickly left with the box and started my crusade to find someone who could possibly free you—one with the goodness of a child and the heart of a lion. In all those hundreds of years, there were only three others for whom I placed the box somewhere they would find it. One was a girl I truly thought would be able to free you. She was so strong. But her parents found the box, read the inscription, and threw it away. I retrieved it quickly, of course, and continued my quest. And then, finally, I found you, Ollie. I will forever be indebted to you and your friends."

Adrian and his mother, Zara, gazed at me. "How can we ever repay you for what you've done for us?" she asked.

"Yes, you have released both of us from a life of misery and loneliness," said Adrian with gratitude.

"Thank you to all three of you," said Zara. "We couldn't have done it without your help."

Mellie and Scotty smiled. "I'm glad it ended this way," said Mellie.

"Yeah, I'm glad the Serpent Witch is gone forever," said Scotty.

I turned to Adrian and Zara. "Thank you for helping us, too," I said. "Without your help, we would have disappeared. No one would have known what happened to us. Aggie would have gone on undetected. She would have continued taking and killing children. You have saved a lot of people."

"At last, it's over." Zara said. She turned to Adrian, "It is time for us to go." Adrian nodded.

"Where will you go?" I asked. I was sad that they had to

leave.

"We will go back in time and find a place where we will live out our lives together. We will take care of each other. Do not worry about us. We are now right where we should be. Together."

"We hate to see you go," I said. "But we understand."

Mellie and Scotty looked sad, too, but nodded in agreement.

"Take care of each other," said Zara. "May your friendship last forever. It will protect you and make you stronger."

"Goodbye, my dearest friends, and many thanks," said Adrian.

"Are you ready, Adrian?" Zara asked, love for him shining brightly from her eyes.

"Yes, Mother," Adrian replied.

Zara held both of his hands in hers. She recited an incantation, and before we knew it, white and gold smoke spun around them. They smiled and waved one more time.

Then they were gone.

I yelled out, "Good luck and thank you!" Mellie and Scotty were waving goodbye.

But Adrian and Zara had disappeared.

CHAPTER 33

A few days later, we met at Mellie's house. There was a lot to talk about. I wanted to make sure we all understood everything that happened.

Mellie gave us some pop, chips, and caramel corn. We weren't supposed to eat a lot of junk food. But we were so relieved and happy about how things had worked out, we decided to celebrate. As we enjoyed the treats Mellie gave us, I remembered something I wanted to check on.

"Something has been bothering me about the baseball we found in Aggie's office," I said. Using Mellie's computer, I brought up the articles about the missing children. I quickly skimmed the articles until I found what I was looking for.

"Here it is," I said as I pointed to the screen.

"What is it?" asked Mellie.

"Did we miss something?" asked Scotty.

"We didn't exactly miss it," I said. "We just didn't know then what we know now. Here look."

Mellie and Scotty peered over my shoulder as I pointed to the list of names of the children that disappeared. "This name,

Johnny Knapp, was one of the missing children. There was a baseball on the bookshelf in Aggie's office with his name on it. I knew it sounded familiar."

"You're right, Ollie. I remember that baseball," Mellie said.

We felt sad about what happened to Johnny Knapp and the rest of them. We could have been on that list.

We tried to tell the police about the missing children, Aggie, Cassandra, and the snakes, but they didn't believe us. I couldn't blame them. I wouldn't have believed it either if I hadn't experienced it.

We showed them the secret room in Aggie's shop with all the stuff she had in there. They said they would check into it, but there wasn't much they could do since they couldn't locate Aggie or Cassandra. They couldn't find any evidence that the snakes ever existed either.

We knew, of course, they all existed.

It was such an unbelievable experience. We had barely survived. I thought we should go over it, to make sure we understood the whole situation. "Let's start at the beginning, with Hagatha and go from there," I said.

Mellie and Scotty nodded. Then Mellie said, "Hagatha was an evil witch who attracted children with sweet treats, trinkets and toys."

"Yes," I agreed. "Like the scarf, baseball cap, and gloves we found."

"Unfortunately," Mellie continued, "once she had them, they were never seen again. She stole their youth and goodness. Once she got what she wanted, she gave the children to her

The Legend of the Serpent Witch

pets. The snakes. Those awful snakes. She continued her evil ways over the centuries."

I thought about it for a minute. "This is just a guess, but I have a theory about why the snake's eyes didn't look right."

"What are you saying, Ollie?" asked Mellie.

"Whatever it is, it's probably going to gross us out," predicted Scotty.

I knew what I was going to tell them was shocking. It was shocking to me too. "I think the snakes' eyes were the eyes of the children they ate."

"Oh, Ollie, that's terrible!" cried Mellie.

"I know," I said. "When we first saw them, I thought for a second that the snakes' eyes looked sad. It happened so fast that I thought I had imagined it. But I hadn't. I don't know how it happened, but the eyes of the children became the snakes' eyes."

"I knew it was going to be something like that," Scotty said knowingly. He rubbed his stomach as if he was feeling sick.

We were quiet for a few minutes. Lost in our own thoughts. Thinking about what could have happened to us. How close we came to a disastrous ending, if not for Adrian's help.

"Without Adrian's help, we would have disappeared like that, too," I said. "We would have been three more missing children, never to be seen again."

"We could have been eaten by the snakes," Scotty said.

"We were lucky," I concluded.

"That's for sure," said Mellie. "Adrian was very brave. And so was Zara. It took great courage to confront Hagatha. She put that horrible curse on Adrian, and then one on Zara, destroying their lives. But Zara never gave up trying to find someone to free Adrian through all the centuries. And then she found you, Ollie. Your goodness helped to release Adrian from his prison box. Then, with the help of all three of us, our goodness destroyed Hagatha."

"I did more research," Mellie continued. "The chant '*Amor et Bonitas Destruet te*' is Latin for 'Love and goodness will destroy you.'"

"That makes sense," I said. "As evil as Hagatha was, she was no match for the love that Adrian and Zara had for each other, along with the goodness the three of us have."

"I didn't know you two *had* any goodness," joked Scotty. "Ouch," he said as Mellie punched his arm.

I smiled. "Hagatha, the Serpent Witch, was finally destroyed. We sent her to hell for all eternity. The mystery of the missing children is solved. What happened to them is heart breaking. But Hagatha can't hurt any more children."

"What a relief," said Scotty.

"I'm glad it's finally over," said Mellie.

"I almost forgot about this." I pulled out the small brown box. "I don't need this anymore."

I opened Mellie's back door and threw it as far as I could into the trees. It landed in dead wet leaves.

"Well," I said, "another mystery solved."

"I'm glad it all worked out so well," said Mellie with a smile.

"Now that's over with, what do you want to do?" asked Scotty. I knew he just wanted to go and have fun.

The Legend of the Serpent Witch

All they needed was one look at me. "Oh no," said Mellie. She knew that I was ready to solve another mystery.

"That figures," said Scotty.

I smiled at them both. I couldn't have better friends. "If you're stuck, keep moving forward," I said, grinning.

EPILOGUE

The night was very quiet. Unusually quiet. The air in the woods was very still. Clouds passed slowly over the moon. For a few minutes, moonlight touched the box.

At first, nothing happened. Then the box began to make a scraping noise. It shook. Black smoke slowly seeped from its cracks. A low creaking groan came from deep inside it. It sounded as if something was trying to open the lid. Then very slowly, the lid started to lift.

More black smoke flew out of the box, as if it were trying to escape from something unimaginable. It spun into the sky, mixing with the dark clouds.

The lid slowly rose a little higher. A long, gray bony finger raised the lid almost off the box.

The finger had lost all its skin. Its long, ragged fingernail was yellowed and broken. Strangely, a tiny piece of skin was beginning to grow back on the finger.

A high-pitched laugh came from inside the box. If one listened very carefully, they would have heard it say, "One day I'll return, and *you will die*, *Evil Destroyer*. You and your friends

The Legend of the Serpent Witch

will be destroyed."

The laughter slowly faded away. The box lid slammed shut.

The wind quickly picked up. Trees started swaying as the wind sharply flew between their branches. Leaves were hurled into the air. Then all was quiet. But there was a menacing presence waiting....anticipating ...

Be on the lookout for the next adventure of Ollie, Mellie, and Scotty in the Scary Shivers series, coming in 2023.